Wave after wave w **fragile raft.**

"Hang on, Grace."

Dakota continued paddling, keeping his eyes on the distant shore up ahead.

"Oh, no." Grace's voice was weak, faraway.

He craned his neck to see what she was looking at behind them. He had only a moment to register that a wave towered above them, blocking his view like a wall of water. The wave descended, crashing over their boat. As though forced by some giant hand, the raft plummeted beneath the water, sending Grace and Dakota to the depths of the ocean.

Dakota struggled beneath the weight of the water and the overwhelming power that had pushed him deeper underwater. He had only minutes to right himself and get to the surface before both he and Grace drowned.

Ever since she found the Nancy Drew books with the pink covers in her country school library, **Sharon Dunn** has loved mystery and suspense. Most of her books take place in Montana, where she lives with three nearly grown children and a hyper border collie. She lost her beloved husband of twenty-seven years to cancer in 2014. When she isn't writing, she loves to hike surrounded by God's beauty.

Books by Sharon Dunn

Love Inspired Suspense

Dead Ringer
Night Prey
Her Guardian
Broken Trust
Zero Visibility
Montana Standoff
Top Secret Identity
Wilderness Target
Cold Case Justice
Mistaken Target
Fatal Vendetta
Big Sky Showdown
Hidden Away
In Too Deep
Wilderness Secrets
Undercover Threat

True Blue K-9 Unit

Courage Under Fire

Texas Ranger Holidays

Thanksgiving Protector

Visit the Author Profile page at Harlequin.com for more titles.

UNDERCOVER THREAT

SHARON DUNN

LOVE INSPIRED SUSPENSE
INSPIRATIONAL ROMANCE

LOVE INSPIRED® SUSPENSE
INSPIRATIONAL ROMANCE

Recycling programs
for this product may
not exist in your area.

ISBN-13: 978-1-335-40280-6

Undercover Threat

Copyright © 2020 by Sharon Dunn

All rights reserved. No part of this book may be used or reproduced in
any manner whatsoever without written permission except in the case of
brief quotations embodied in critical articles and reviews.

This is a work of fiction. Names, characters, places and incidents are either the
product of the author's imagination or are used fictitiously. Any resemblance
to actual persons, living or dead, businesses, companies, events or locales is
entirely coincidental.

This edition published by arrangement with Harlequin Books S.A.

For questions and comments about the quality of this book,
please contact us at CustomerService@Harlequin.com.

Love Inspired
22 Adelaide St. West, 40th Floor
Toronto, Ontario M5H 4E3, Canada
www.Harlequin.com

Printed in U.S.A.

Weeping may endure for a night,
but joy cometh in the morning.
–Psalm 30:5

I cried by reason of mine affliction unto the Lord, and
he heard me; out of the belly of hell cried I, and thou
heardest my voice. For thou hadst cast me into the
deep, in the midst of the seas; and floods compassed me
about: all thy billows and thy waves passed over me.
–Jonah 2:2-3

For Shannon, who brings so much humor and adventure into my life. So glad you are my son.

ONE

Undercover Drug Enforcement agent Grace Young stepped into the dark galley of the cruise ship where she was working as a cook. She took in a deep breath to try to release some tension in her body. The anonymous note had said to meet in the kitchen at midnight. The rest of the crew and passengers were sound asleep.

Since being hired on, Grace had dropped hints of how cash-strapped she was. She'd implied that she'd had brushes with the law. Would this meeting be her "in" for finding out how drugs, mostly meth, were being manufactured in Seattle, trafficked up through Canada and then brought back into the United States via the northern border? DEA had traced most of the transport to one particular cruise line that did tours of the San Juan Islands and Canada. Whether the owner of the cruise line, Mitchell Wilson, was involved or if someone who worked for the cruise line was running the operation was not clear. Only Grace's undercover work could ferret that out.

She tuned her ears to her surroundings, hearing only the creaking of the ship. Wind had picked up and the ship was lilting side to side at a more extreme angle. A storm was moving in. She reached for the light switch.

A hand went over her mouth.

Hot lava breath pummeled her ear. "I know what you're up to."

Had her cover been blown? How would he have found out? If so, she was a dead woman. Her heartbeat drummed in her ears. She didn't recognize the man's voice. This was a small ship with a crew of only fifteen and forty passengers. His voice was generic in character.

The man wrapped an arm around her waist and drew her even closer. She felt pressure on her stomach, making it hard to breathe.

She tried to twist free.

"No one horns in on my game, you hear me?"

So her cover wasn't blown. This guy just didn't want to share his illegal cash cow with anyone. Was he the only operator for this leg of the trafficking? "You mean to tell me you're the only one who gets to see some green from this little gig of yours? Come on, share the wealth."

"I don't know who you've been talking to or what you know but stay out."

She relaxed a little. Maybe he was just going to warn her and let her go.

"I can tell you love to run your mouth." He pressed his lips close to her ear again. "You're going to tell someone what I've been doing, aren't you?"

Fear came back tenfold. His voice was filled with murderous rage. She shook her head even as her heart pounded.

"I'll make sure you don't," he said.

His words chilled her to the bone. He was probably going to kill her and throw her overboard. She had to get away. She kicked him hard in the shin.

He released his hold and she whirled around. He pulled a gun out from his waistband. It had a silencer on it. No one would hear the shot.

Though it was dark, she recognized him as one of the crew members who worked above deck, not someone she interacted with much. She knew him by first name only, Joe.

They stood staring at each other. He raised the gun so the red dot laser sight landed on her chest.

Her heart raced. She put a protective hand out as if that would stop the bullet. "If I disappear that will raise a red flag to the authorities. You don't want the cops sniffing around, do you?"

She took a step back toward the counter, remembering that she had taken an open bag of flour out of the pantry to make biscuits in the morning.

He sneered and stepped toward her, still aiming the gun at her chest. "They'll never find your body. I'll just tell a story about what a druggie you were. That you probably fell overboard."

She spun, grabbed the bag of flour off the counter and tossed it at him. It hit him square in the head, creating a cloud around him. The move seemed to stun him. He'd dropped the gun.

She turned and raced toward the door to get down the hall where the rest of the crew slept. She'd wake the captain, tell him this man had tried to rob her at gunpoint. He'd be taken into custody at the next port. The ruse would buy her time and maybe keep her cover intact.

He gave up looking for the gun and blocked her way to the hallway.

She did an about-face and sprinted toward the stairs. She had no choice but to go on deck where the passengers slept in their rooms. She'd have to bang on doors and raise a ruckus.

She ran halfway up the stairs.

A hand with an iron grip wrapped around her ankle and dragged her back down. She twisted around and kicked him in the face. The move was enough to paralyze him for a moment. She flipped over and bolted up the stairs.

He was right at her heels, reaching out to grasp her shirt hem. She pulled away.

She sprinted to get above deck. The ship rocked and swayed, and the wind blew around her. The storm was picking up. He did not come right after her, which meant he must have gone back for the gun.

She'd taken two steps toward the long corridor that led to where the passengers were sleeping in their rooms when he grabbed her from behind. She spun around to defend herself so she could escape. He must have put the gun in his waistband again. Maybe he was afraid of witnesses. People might be awake because of the storm. Otherwise, he would have shot her in the back.

He clamped his hands around her neck, squeezing. She tried to push him away by pressing her hand against his chest. She pinched his pectoral muscle, not exactly in the DEA training manual, but it worked. He let go.

The ship continued to sway, tilting at a severe angle. They both fell and slid across the deck as a spray of water hit her. The storm was getting worse. The captain must have been at the helm by now even if crew members hadn't been pulled out of bed yet. Could she get to him before this man shot her or threw her overboard? Maybe she should just scream for help, though she doubted she would be heard above the noise of the storm.

They both rose to their feet. She tried to find her balance on the unsteady platform. Joe stalked toward her. He clamped his hand on the front of her neck and pushed her until her back was against the railing of the ship. Again, he tried to choke her, trapping her in with his other hand. She clawed at his hands. She could feel herself getting light-headed. In her peripheral vision, she saw the high rolling waves coming toward the ship. Hitting the side. Splashing across the deck.

"Something wrong here?" The voice sounded very far away.

Joe let up on the hold he had on her neck.

On the far side of the deck the crew member who had called out to her, whose name she did not know, had emerged, probably to deal with issues connected to the storm.

"He tried to hurt me!" She was shouting to be heard above the intensity of the waves and wind, but it felt like her words fell at her feet.

Joe took the gun out and pointed it at the other crew member, who put his hands up. They all had to put their energy into not falling. None of them had solid footing on the rocking ship. She lunged toward Joe, intending to snag the gun away from him. An innocent man didn't need to die. The two wrestled with the gun. The crew member disappeared around a corner. He would get help. This would all be over soon.

Joe hit her across the jaw with the gun. She stumbled backward against the railing.

He aimed the gun at her. He must have known he had only minutes before he'd be found out. She braced for the impact of the bullet. A wave came up, washing over her and the entire ship. She felt herself being lifted up and then sucked underwater. She surfaced long enough to get a breath. She'd been pulled overboard by the wave.

She caught a glimpse of Joe anchoring himself by clinging to the railing before another wave covered her.

The ship drew farther away as more waves hit it. It was lilting to one side. Something wasn't right with the ship.

It must have been taking on water.

She tried to swim but the waves crashed against her, hitting her body with such force it was like being hit with liquid rocks.

The last thing she saw was Joe cutting the dinghy loose and getting into it. He knew he'd been caught. Was he going to try to get away or come after her? Maybe both.

As she struggled to stay above water, she wondered if she might die. In a way, maybe that would be relief from the pain she'd been trying to outrun. She'd been taking dangerous assignments ever since her two-year-old daughter had died and her marriage had fallen apart as a result three years ago.

Another waved crashed over her, pulling her under. She struggled for air, slicing her arms through the weight of the water to try to get back to the surface. She didn't want to die.

Was there a God? Would He hear her if she cried out to Him?

* * *

Coast Guard rescue swimmer Dakota Young stood at the edge of the helicopter ready for his drop. He searched the turbulent waters surrounding the San Juan Islands. The storm had come up with a vicious intensity. Way beyond what the forecast had predicted.

They'd received calls of boats taking on water. And of people tossed overboard. He surveyed the ocean below. He saw a man in a motorized dinghy and then a smaller object in the water caught his eye. "There." He pointed. His was trained to discern the gray of the water from the color of a person's head and arms. At this distance, he couldn't tell if the person in peril was male or female. They would rescue the man in the dinghy but the person in the water was priority. He watched as the person, aware of the helicopter, tilted his or her head for just a moment before being covered by another wave.

The helicopter dropped in altitude. Wind gusted against the body, rocking it.

Dakota took in a breath that contained a silent prayer. This was not going to be an easy drop. Though he had not been raised a Christian, he'd found a deep faith during his training with the Coast Guard. The life-and-death situations the men and women faced made them cling to each other and to God.

The pilot's voice reverberated in the radio in Dakota's ear. "That's as close as I can get."

The chopper jerked from the force of the wind. Dakota gave the pilot the thumbs-up and he nodded at the other two crew members. Dressed in a dry suit and flippers, Dakota made the leap into the roiling dark waters. He hit the surface and plunged beneath, trusting that his body would naturally rise back up.

Now he could see that he was dealing with a woman. She was clinging to a piece of wood or plastic; he couldn't tell exactly what it was. She tried to ride the waves as they rolled over her. As he stroked through the water, he had a view of only the back of her head, her long hair soaked and stringy. She turned, her expression growing wide with recognition. He almost didn't believe what he was seeing. The woman in the water was his ex-wife, Grace.

Dakota was transported back to three years ago. His marriage had fallen apart after the death of their little girl, Anita. Grace had become depressed. At first, he had poured himself into his work as a DEA agent. They drifted apart. Once the divorce was final, he'd joined the Coast Guard knowing that he had to do something that was more life-giving. He hadn't seen his ex-wife in three years.

He swam toward her. "Grace, I'm going to get you out of here."

Already the chopper was lowering the rescue basket, though the high winds made it a challenge to achieve any degree of accuracy.

Her hand touched his cheek briefly. "Dakota. How strange that it should be you." He suspected there was a whole story around her comment but now was not the time to find out.

She was shivering, cold and wet. If hypothermia had not set in, it would soon. He could only guess at how long she'd been in the cold waters.

She was still clinging to the wooden board. He had to shout above the roar of the waves. "Let go of the board and hold on to me."

She wrapped an arm around his shoulder, then he

stroked toward where the rescue basket was still being whipped around in the wind. They drew closer. Hours of exercise and training gave him the stamina he needed to tow Grace and still make progress through the waves.

Well trained to stay calm in perilous situations, she clung to him. If she had fought him by flailing out of panic as some victims did, he might have to let go until she calmed enough so she didn't take them both under. That was the hardest part of rescue.

Above the wind and the crashing waves, a different kind of noise reached his ears, a sort of piercing zing. He glanced across the water, shocked to see the man in a motorized dinghy taking aim at them. The man fired several times.

Dakota was within five feet of the rescue basket. The chopper jiggled and then slanted to one side.

Through his earpiece radio, Dakota heard the pilot's panicked voice. "Got some sort of engine failure. Maybe damage from the storm. Will limp back to base. Pray we make it. Calling for help. Someone will come for you."

The pilot must have been so focused on his job that he hadn't noticed the man in the dinghy shooting at them.

Smoke swirled from the helicopter motor as a mechanical grinding noise replaced the smooth hum of the engine. A package was pushed out of the chopper. Dakota knew that they had provided whatever they could to help him.

The chopper turned and twisted, still dragging the rescue basket. Islands in the sound were within sight but still some distance away. He prayed they would find safe landing before the motor gave out if they couldn't get back to base.

Grace screamed as the man fired yet another shot. Dakota worked his way toward where the chopper had dropped something, trying to put distance between himself and the shooter.

He glanced over his shoulder just as a huge wave knocked the man out of the boat. The chopper had dropped an inflatable raft. Letting go of Grace, Dakota pulled the cord. Even before it was fully inflated, he reached out for Grace and lifted her into the craft. She was clearly weak from her struggle.

The other boat looked as though it had been battered and damaged by the waves that had taken the shooter under. The man had not yet bobbed to the surface.

Dakota crawled into the raft as well. Both of them lay on their stomachs gasping for air. Waves continued to rock the boat as water sprayed across the bow. He pulled himself into a sitting position and grabbed the oar that was attached to the inner wall of the craft. The waves were so strong he had very little control despite his strength and skill. Water cascaded into the boat. Grace clung to the safety rope, still lying on her stomach.

The rain came down with such power, it looked like gray sheets hung from the sky. He could barely make out the helicopter in the distance. It seemed to be sputtering and shaking, losing and gaining altitude at random. They were close to a tree-covered island. The chopper disappeared into the gloom created by the rain and then his radio cut out. He had no idea if they had been able to land or had simply crashed.

Help would come for them all. But right now, he needed to get Grace to dry land where she would be safe and warm. He steered the boat toward the island, not sure what he would find there. Neither the man who had shot at them nor his boat was anywhere in the inky turbulent waters.

Wave after wave washed over their fragile raft.

"Hang on, Grace."

He continued paddling, keeping his eyes on the distant shore up ahead.

"Oh, no." Grace's voice was weak, faraway.

He craned his neck to see behind at what she was looking at. He had only a moment to register that a wave towered above them, blocking his view like a wall of water. The wave descended, crashing over their boat. As though forced by some giant hand, the raft plummeted beneath the water, sending Grace and Dakota to the depths of the ocean.

Dakota struggled beneath the weight of the water and the overwhelming power that had pushed him deeper underwater. He had only minutes to right himself and get to the surface before both he and Grace drowned.

TWO

Once again, Grace had the sense that she was powerless against the forces of nature. It was as if a vacuum sucked her down while the weight of the water pushed from above. She lost all orientation to where she was in space. She flailed her arms trying to find the water's surface.

God, please, if You are real, I don't want to die.

A force grabbed her shirt collar and jerked her up. And then arms wrapped around her waist. Dakota had found her in the depths. Weak from the fight, she was a rag doll in his arms. He kicked and used his free arm to break through the surface of the water. Both of them gasped for air.

The wave had pushed them closer to the shore. She could barely see the large boulders on the beach and beyond that the evergreens. The overcast sky made the darkness seem even blacker. With Dakota doing most of the work, they made their way closer to shore until the water was shallow enough for Dakota to stand up in. Rain sprinkled on them as they reached the rocky shore.

Dakota helped her to her feet. Her knees buckled when she tried to stand on her own. He gathered her up and held her in his arms as he carried her around the large boulders and into the trees. She shivered. His dry suit kept him warm, but she was wearing street clothes. He sat her down so her back was up against a tree. The canopy of the trees kept the rain out. She was coherent enough to understand that her body was going into hypothermia.

He put both his hands on her cheeks. "Stay with me. Don't give up."

She nodded. When they'd worked together as DEA agents, Dakota had always had her back.

He unzipped the front of his dry suit and patted his chest, meaning his body heat would help warm her up. He helped her get out of the thin, soaked jacket she had on and then drew her close.

There was a time when she had loved being held by him. And yes, given that they had no other option, this was the best solution to warm her up again. He rubbed her arms as she pressed close to him. She could feel his heartbeat against her ear.

She was so cold she was vibrating like a washing machine with an unbalanced load. Shivering was good; it meant her body was still trying to fight the cold. Once hypothermia took hold, brain fog would make it hard for her to even cogitate what was happening as her organs started to shut down.

That she'd had such an intense exposure to cold and wet and was still coherent felt like an answer to her desperate prayer.

"Better?" Dakota's chest vibrated when he spoke.

She nodded. "Think so." Her teeth were still chattering.

He pulled away. "We need to get you warmed up

faster." He tore his flippers off and slipped out of his dry suit, stripping down to his swimming trunks and T-shirt. "Get into this. It will warm you up faster."

"But you're going to be cold."

"Do what I say, Grace." He rose to his feet.

When he used that tone of voice, she knew not to argue with him. He was trying to keep her alive.

He shoved the dry suit toward her.

"Thank you," she said.

"While you change, I'm going to try to figure out where we are and how to get the rescue crew's attention. If they can get out at all, they will be looking for us."

That was a big *if*…

"I'm worried to about that guy who shot at us. He might still come after us." He turned to go but then pivoted to look at her. "Sit tight. Do not move because I need to be able to find you. I'll be back. I promise. I thought I saw a flashing light when we were out on the water. I think there might be a lighthouse on the island."

She watched as he took off running, barefoot. He disappeared into the thickness of the evergreens.

Grace pulled off her soggy canvas shoes and got into the dry suit. She zipped it up. The warmth enveloped her. Dakota was six inches taller than her. The bottoms of the legs of the suit covered her feet almost to the ends of her toes. She wrapped her arms around her body and sat back down against the tree. The shivering stopped. Her head cleared.

Dakota was out in the elements trying to find a way to get to safety with hardly any covering to keep him warm. He was willing to take risks to help her even though it had been three years since she'd seen him. After the divorce, he'd quit the DEA. They couldn't work together anymore. She heard through mutual friends that he'd joined the Coast Guard. Still, seeing him swimming toward her in the water had been a shock almost as severe as the cold and wet.

She had no idea where they were. They might even be connected to the mainland, though more likely they were on an island. She drew her knees up to her chest. Though her muscles were heavy with fatigue, she was no longer cold. She brushed her long wet hair off her face.

She startled when she heard noises. Something moving through the trees from the shore side, not where Dakota had gone. Some kind of wildlife, maybe?

The wind continued to blow, causing the branches at the top of the trees to creak and sway. She didn't hear any more sounds.

She focused on her own breathing and the hardness of the tree as she pressed her back against it. She was grateful to be warmed up again but worried about Dakota being affected by the cold. A flash of movement in the trees off to the side caught her attention. She studied each tree trunk, separating them out but not seeing or hearing anything out of place. The silence fell around her like a heavy blanket. Only the creaking of the topmost branches as they fought with the wind reached her ears.

Her heart beat a little faster as she rose to her feet and stretched her hand back for the support of the tree. Even though she couldn't see anything, she couldn't shake the feeling that she was being watched. She was a trained agent. That meant she needed to trust her instincts. Most threats were detected at the gut level before the senses even registered them.

After pulling up the legs of the dry suit so she wouldn't trip, she took a step to the side, turned and ran in the direction that Dakota had gone. Her bare feet padded through the forest floor. Moss provided some softness, though twigs and tiny rocks dug into her feet. She glanced over her shoulder. Again, there was no sensory evidence to suggest she was not alone, but the prickling of the hairs on the back of her neck told her otherwise.

She ran through the evergreens, guessing at which path Dakota had taken. Once she was free of the trees, the wind whipped around her. The sky thundered and flashed as lightning struck the turbulent dark water. She had a view of only one shoreline, which meant the island might be quite large.

Though she was barefoot, her strength had been renewed by being warmed up. She broke into a run. The terrain was rolling hills with only brush and grass. When she had run some distance, she turned back around, looking at the trees where she had just come from. Again, she saw movement, a glimpse of color that stood out from the trees, and then nothing. Whoever was back there did not want to be seen and had taken cover behind a tree.

It was most likely Joe, the man who had shot at her. With the severity of the storm, there were probably plenty of people who had been tossed overboard or had jumped from sinking ships. But a survivor from another ship or even the one she'd been on would just show him or herself, relieved at seeing another person. Whoever was out there didn't want to reveal himself.

She ran faster. Grass and pebbles poked the bottoms of her feet.

How was she ever going to figure out where Dakota had gone? He wasn't anywhere out in the open. The grassy terrain dipped down and then rose up toward another cluster of trees. He must have gone there. She reached the edge of trees just as the rain sprinkling from the sky turned into a downpour. More thunder cracked against her ears. She scanned the forest, desperate to locate Dakota.

Dakota hurried back through the trees. He'd run far enough to have a view of a distant shore where he'd spotted a lighthouse. Most lighthouses these days were automated. So far, he'd seen no other signs of habitation on the island. The lighthouse would at least provide some shelter and maybe some way to contact help. He glanced back at the roiling dark waters that surrounded the island. Thunder crackled and lighting lit up the sky. Help might not be able to get to them until the storm broke up.

The mossy forest floor moist from spring rain was almost spongy beneath his feet. Right now, his focus was on keeping Grace safe.

He hurried through the tall trees. Moss grew everywhere, weighing down branches and covering trunks. Once he was beneath the protection of the trees, not much rain fell on him. Still, he was cold from exposure and fatigued from the exertion of the swim and then run. He sprinted through the trees.

He heard his name called, though it sounded very far away. Grace.

"Over here." With the wind so intense, he wasn't sure his voice would carry far. He ran in the general direction the sound had come from. Why had she left the spot he'd asked her to stay in?

"Dakota."

"Here, Grace. I'm right here." He corrected the direction he'd been going. He slowed, trying to see through all the green of the trees and moss. "Grace?"

She burst through the trees and fell into his arms.

"Hey, what's going on?"

"I think someone else is here with us."

He shook his head. "Yours wasn't the only ship to send out a distress signal."

She tilted her head. "He didn't come out into the open."

He remembered the man with the gun. Grace had a lot of explaining to do but now was not the time. He could only assume that it was connected to her work with the DEA. He'd heard through mutual friends that she was doing undercover work. When Anita was born, they had both agreed that undercover work was too dangerous. They didn't want to leave their child an orphan. How strange life had turned out. "Are you sure you saw someone?"

"Just a gut feeling I got. You remember those, don't you?"

"Sure."

"And then I'm almost sure I saw movement in the trees, a human not an animal," she said.

"I trust your judgment." He studied her. He thought he saw trust in her blue eyes. The years they'd been together, snapshots of memories, flashed through his mind. They had been good together. "I spotted a lighthouse. We should go there." He pointed. "This way up the hill."

She fell in beside him. Though both were barefoot, they ran as fast as they could as the rain fell on them. He glanced over his shoulder, not seeing anyone. If there was someone else on the island, he wanted to stay out of sight.

It could be that it wasn't the man with the gun but someone who had suffered a head injury in the fall from a boat and did not have very good survival skills. Even as the thought ran through his brain, he realized how far-fetched it seemed. If Grace had seen someone, and he had not shown himself, he was probably hostile.

They sprinted up the hill and down into a valley. The grove of trees they passed through provided some shelter and escape from the wind and rain.

Grace slowed down. "How far is it?"

He stopped and turned to face her. "I saw the light-house from the top of the next hill, but it's all the way across the island. Five miles, I would guess." Her drooping shoulders and sagging features suggested weariness. He reached out to touch her arm. "I know it's a ways, but it's our best option. Battling the ocean wore us both out. Can you make it?"

She nodded. "You're the one who's dressed for a beach party. You must be cold."

He was chilled, but she didn't need to know that. "I'm all right." He didn't want to add to her list of concerns. "Come on, Gracie Girl, let's go."

Her expression changed as though a shadow had fallen over her face. When they were married, Gracie Girl had been his nickname for her. Something no one else called her. He'd used the endearment out of habit, not to upset her.

"Sorry."

She shrugged. "Let's focus on getting to that light-house."

They continued through the forest and up the next hill. The storm continued to stir up the waters around them.

They ran and rested and kept running until they were too tired to jog and then they walked as the lighthouse drew closer. His feet touched the stone walkway that led to the lighthouse entrance. He was shivering and wet. They stood at the doorway of the lighthouse, where a placard was hung. As he suspected, the lighthouse was automated. At least he knew where they were now: on Patos Island.

"I guess they'll understand if we break in, huh?" Grace stood beside him on the cement slab outside the door. He could hear the fatigue in her voice.

He reached for the doorknob. "Some of these places are set up for tourists or for people in distress." The knob turned and the door creaked open.

He gestured for her to go first and then he stepped in behind her. They entered a small room that had more placards and a wall with photos designed to give tour-ists the history of the island. There were two doors. He found a room with a sink and toilet. When he tried the other door it was locked, which meant it probably led up to the lighthouse tower, not something the general public would have access to without a ranger around.

Grace peered into the bathroom. "We can get a drink of water at least." She stepped into the bathroom. He could hear her opening and shutting cupboard doors on the vanity and then another that had been on the far wall.

"Probably just cleaning supplies," he said.

"It's worth a try." Another cupboard slammed. She stepped back out into the room holding a plastic tub filled with jackets, shirts and hats. She smiled triumphantly. "The lost and found of Patos Island."

Her smile could still lift his spirits even in the most trying of circumstances. "Good job."

She sat the tub down and rooted through it until she found a sweatshirt with the words *World's Greatest Grandma* emblazoned on it. "That looks like about your size." She tossed it toward him.

He held it up. "And such a fitting moniker."

She released a small laugh.

"So glad there are plus-size grandmothers in the world, huh?"

They both laughed. They took turns going into the bathroom to change into dry clothes.

After they got a drink of water, they settled down with their backs against the wall. Grace made a blanket with the remaining clothes. He sat down beside her but a few inches from her.

She tilted her head toward the ceiling. "I guess now we can't do anything but wait for that storm to pass."

Now that they were not fighting the elements, he sensed a tension between them. The moment of levity they'd shared seemed to vanish.

Even if the Coast Guard braved the storm, they would have no way of knowing where they'd ended up. He wondered if his brothers in the chopper had made it back to base or had to crash-land. They were probably going to be here for a while. Might as well try to make conversation.

"You could tell me what you were doing out there. Why that man shot a gun at you. Undercover work?"

"Actually, Dakota, I can't tell you. It's classified."

A chill seemed to enter the room. There had been a time when they'd shared everything about work.

"I get it. I'm sorry. I'm not DEA anymore."

"No, you're not."

And he wasn't her husband anymore either. Pain stabbed at his heart. She was the one who had filed for divorce. Maybe he had been working longer hours to run from the grief of losing Anita while she had taken a leave of absence, sleeping sixteen hours a day. Neither one of them had been there for the other. He saw that now.

He thought for a moment before he spoke up. "I'm glad you were able to go back to work."

"I had bills to pay. I had to."

"But undercover work, it's so dangerous," he said. "I worry about you."

"It's not your job to worry about me anymore." She tugged on one of the jackets that covered her legs. "It's my choice."

"Just promise me you don't have a death wish, because for a long time I think I did. It scared me. That's why I got out of the DEA."

"I don't have a death wish, okay? Can we talk about something else?"

The conversation wasn't going as he'd hoped. He wanted to tell her about the healing he'd found and the God he knew because of the Coast Guard. "Sorry, I seem to be putting my foot in my mouth." It appeared that the pain of their past was just beneath the surface for her.

"I thought you got out of the DEA so you wouldn't have to run into me," she said. Her words tinged with pain.

"No, if that was the case, I could have put in for a transfer to a different office."

"Dakota, I appreciate you trying to talk to me. But maybe we should just rest until the storm breaks."

"Sure." He rose to his feet and stepped toward the door. He clicked the dead bolt on it. "Just in case that person you saw in the trees catches up with us." He turned to face her, seeing fear in her eyes.

He sat down beside her a little closer than before. She didn't pull away from him. He closed his eyes. "I'm sorry. I don't see you for three years and the first thing I do is tell you how to live your life."

Her voice softened. "It's okay." She lay down using one of the articles of clothing as a pillow. Her back was turned toward him.

He rested his head on the cold hard floor, allowing sleep to overtake him. Of all the Coast Guard swimmers who could have been sent out on the call to save Grace, he had been the one to arrive to save her. He didn't think that was a coincidence. It had to be God.

Hours later, the sound of breaking glass and the smell of fire roused him from his slumber. Several flaming items were thrown through the broken window. The room looked like a series of campfires, all increasing in intensity. Smoke filled the air, stinging his eyes. He jumped to his feet ready to battle the consuming flames.

THREE

A smell tickled Grace's nose. She awoke with a start. Flames and heat were in front of her. Three burning objects on the floor. A pamphlet rack low to the ground had caught fire.

Dakota was on his feet even as the room filled with smoke. He glanced around for something to smother the fire with. He couldn't stomp on it with his bare feet.

Grace jumped up, grabbing a bandanna that had been in the pile of clothing. She tore it in half as she ran toward the bathroom. She wet both pieces.

She shoved a bucket used for cleaning in the sink and turned on the water. Dakota coughed. The flames traveled up the rack of brochures, consuming the paper. A chemical smell filled the air; the plastic that covered the wire rack was melting.

She handed him the wet bandanna and put the other half over her mouth and nose. After grabbing a small wastebasket, she ran back to the bathroom to get the bucket, which was half full. She put the basket under the tap and carried the bucket toward the fire. Dakota knocked the burning rack of brochures to the floor. She remembered one of the jackets in the lost-and-found pile that looked like it was made of wool. She grabbed it and put it on one of the burning brochures.

The smoke seemed to be everywhere. She retrieved the basket filled with water and placed the bucket under the running tap. She continued the process until all the flames had been extinguished.

Dakota stood back, out of breath and coughing. Smoke still filled the room.

This had to be the work of the man who'd been hiding in the trees, probably Joe from the boat. How he'd found something dry to start a fire with she could only guess. Maybe he'd had a lighter on him.

As the smoke settled and the scent of charred and burnt objects filled the air, she wheezed in a deep breath. "That was something, huh?"

In the dimness she could barely make out Dakota's expression, but he nodded. His body went rigid as he drew his attention to the windows. Flames were shooting up behind them.

Heart pounding, panic kicking into high gear, she ran toward the broken window. She peered out, careful not to touch the glass because it might have been hot. Outside, the flames were at about waist level. Something flammable had been stacked in front of the door. The fire had risen up the door past the doorknob. Joe must have smeared or poured something highly combustible on the door.

Dakota bolted toward the door that led to the tower. "He's trying to either burn us alive or smoke us out. We have to find another way out." He rattled the locked door and then began to search around in the dim light, probably for something to break the lock.

She ran toward the pile of clothes, holding the wet

bandanna over her mouth. She picked up a jacket, twisted it into a ball and shoved it into the place where the window had been broken. Still coughing, she grabbed a T-shirt, ran it under the tap and stuffed it under the door that led outside. The wooden door was warm to the touch. She knew enough not to touch the metal knob. At least now no more smoke would get inside.

Dakota continued to root around behind a display counter. "If I can just find something heavy enough to break the lock."

"Even if we get up to the top of the tower, he can burn us out," she said.

"It will take a while for the flames to travel up the stairs. We can find a way to crawl down," he said. "He has no way of knowing if we've gone up there." He hurried into the bathroom to continue his search. He shouted at her from the next room. "He will think we died of smoke inhalation in here."

She stared outside at the rabid flames. If they opened the door, the wall of flame might consume them. Even if they got through the fire, Joe would be waiting for them, ready to attack. They had no option but to go up.

Dakota returned holding what looked like a wrench. Probably used to repair the plumbing under the sink. Over and over he beat on the doorknob. When it didn't budge, he hit the door with the wrench even harder. The pounding continued while she watched the flames outside growing higher and higher.

A shadowy figure emerged from the darkness, tossing something liquid on the fire, causing the flames to eat away even more of the door. She screamed when another pane of the window burst. A heavy object fell only feet from her. Glass scattered across the floor. Smoke circled in through the new hole.

Dakota had not been wrong. There had been a time in her life when she had wanted to die to be with her baby. Maybe that was why she took the dangerous assignments. She coughed as smoke filled her lungs. "Hurry. We don't have much time." She bent over. She didn't want to die. She knew that now. Again, she called out to a God she wasn't even sure she believed in.

Please, God, help us escape.

Dakota had all but shredded the door. He reached through the splintered hole, trying to undo the locking mechanism. He nearly tore the door off its hinges flinging it open. He turned and reached out toward her.

She was still doubled over from coughing. The smoke was so thick she almost couldn't see. His hand found hers and he pulled her up the narrow winding stairs. Dakota closed what was left of the door behind him. With the thick smoke and the darkness there was no way the arsonist would know they had escaped up to the tower. He coughed. The rising smoke was an issue. They needed to escape and fast.

She hurried up the metal stairs to the large round room where the beacon light flashed. Once again, the god she wasn't even sure was real had saved her…for now. The first time she'd prayed, Dakota had shown up. Of all the Coast Guard swimmers who could have taken the call, it was her ex-husband.

"We have to get out of here." Her throat was scratchy from the smoke. Her sinuses were thick with mucus.

Dakota was already pacing around the circular space. "We can break out a window and climb down."

"Climb down with what?" She glanced around, spotting only a toolbox. It was too much to hope that there would be rope or bedsheets or anything to use to scale down the side of the lighthouse.

Joe was likely on the other side of the lighthouse watching the fire. Eventually, it would burn through the wooden door and travel up the stairs. The stairs were metal and wouldn't burn. Most people didn't die from fire itself; smoke was the bigger concern, and it traveled faster than fire. They had to get out of here as quickly as possible.

Dakota peered through the window. "We don't need to break it." He twisted a latch and pushed the window outward. "Look, I can see a natural harbor out there. Maybe some boats anchored to get out of the storm."

She came and stood beside him. Trees partially covered the view of the cove where boats could come in. Maybe a boat was hidden behind there, but that really didn't help them right now. They were still trapped in the lighthouse. She turned her attention to the ground below. "How are we going to get out of here? We can't jump. At the very least our legs would be broken."

"There's a lookout landing halfway down. We aim for that." He gestured for her to come toward him. "Crawl through. I'll hold your wrists and lower you down."

She looked again. The landing was small and made of black metal. She hadn't noticed it at first. The lighthouse had at one time been a home to the lighthouse keeper. The little lookout probably connected to a door that had led to living quarters. It was a small balcony, maybe two feet by three feet. She lifted her leg and crawled through. She grasped the windowsill while Dakota held her wrists.

Her legs swung, scraping the wall. Panic rose up, causing a sour taste in her mouth. "I can't see down below me."

"I've got you, Gracie Girl. I'll lower you straight down. Tell me when you touch the landing with your toes."

Her heart squeezed tight. Only Dakota called her Gracie. She tilted her foot hoping her toes would find the hard surface. "There. I feel it."

He let go of her. She turned to face toward the ocean. The rain had stopped but the wind continued to whip around her. Waves crashed against the rocks.

She could smell the smoke from the fire. The front door that was on fire was on the other side of the light-house, not the side that faced the water where the look-out landing was. She didn't see anyone. That didn't mean Joe wasn't watching. Once they were on the ground, it would be two against one. He had to have lost the gun when his boat capsized. Still, a confrontation didn't seem like a good idea. He'd found a way to start a fire—maybe he'd found a weapon as well, a hammer or an ax.

She moved to the edge of the landing.

Dakota said, "Tell me if I'm going to miss it."

He lowered himself down. She guided his feet. "Straight down."

He let go of the windowsill and landed hard. The entire balcony creaked. It was old and designed for only one person to be on it.

"I'm going to go down first just in case he's out there," said Dakota. "I don't want him jumping you."

She wanted to remind him that she was a trained agent. But honestly, she liked his idea. She didn't have the energy to get into a fight. Dakota lifted his foot over the metal railing and swung down, dropping to the ground. She waited.

He shout-whispered up to her. "It looks clear."

She held on to the metal bars of the railing.

"Let go, I got you," he said from below.

The drop was maybe ten feet. She released the grip she had on the bars. Dakota caught her as she fell, holding her waist and guiding her to the ground. She turned to face him, resting her palm against his chest. They stood frozen for a few seconds. The gesture was one she'd done a thousand times when they were married. He was standing close enough that when he exhaled, she could feel his breath on her forehead. A rush of memories both good and bad flooded through her mind.

She cleared her throat and took a step back. "We better get to that harbor before he figures out we escaped."

"We could try to take him out. There are two of us. You have the authority to take him into custody."

"I don't want to risk him getting away and knowing that I'm DEA," she whispered. "Hopefully, my cover hasn't been compromised. I want to see this investigation to the end."

"Then let's make a run for it." He grabbed her hand and jogged in the direction of the trees that would lead to the cove. They circled in a wide arc around the back side of the lighthouse, staying low and seeking the cover of some bushes. They came to what looked like a storage shed. The doors were flung wide open. There was a lawn mower and other groundskeeping equipment inside. That explained where Joe had gotten the gasoline to start the fire.

She glanced off to the side where the lighthouse was.

Were the shadows she saw a man moving around or just her imagination?

Dakota tugged on her sleeve. "Keep going. Stay low and move slow."

The distance between the shed and the trees was substantial. If Joe was watching from the shadows, they would be spotted. Maybe his attention was still on the fire and maybe he had seen them scaling down the lighthouse. She had to assume that Joe was still after them.

Both of them dropped to the ground. Dakota was watching the area around the lighthouse as well. They sprinted the final distance to the trees, which grew at a downward slant leading to the cove. She reached out for branches and plants to keep from falling and rolling down the incline. Dakota as well slowed his pace.

The roar of the ocean waves reached her ears and she smelled salt air long before the sandy beach of the cove came into view. The water in the cove was far from calm. She took in a deep breath when she saw a small craft anchored there being bounced by the waves. The boat was maybe a twenty-footer. Big enough to have a below-deck area for sleeping, eating and storage. The kind people took out for short runs.

They stepped out from the forest. No lights were on in the boat. Both of them slowed down.

"Maybe they're trying to conserve their electrical," she said.

"And maybe the boat's been here for a long time… abandoned for whatever reason."

The boat was far enough from shore that they would have to swim out to it in the turbulent waters to even board it.

A sound in the forest behind her, the crackling of a

branch, caused her to whirl around. Her heart beat faster and she stepped a little closer to Dakota. He touched her back and drew her close protectively.

"Let's find a hiding place," he whispered as he pointed to the other side of the cove.

The soft sand of the beach turned to small pebbles as they ran past the boat toward the trees. They were still barefoot. Both of them slipped into the shelter of the trees.

"Something is off with that boat," said Dakota. "I don't see a dinghy on it, which makes me wonder if whoever was on it rowed ashore and is waiting the storm out in the forest. Why does this feel suspicious to me?"

"It doesn't have to be nefarious. It's possible that someone was just out boating when the storm came up and this was the nearest place they could get to." She watched the boat, seeing no sign of life. "Right?"

"Doesn't your gut tell you something else is going on? I suppose they could have thought staying on the boat was unsafe."

"My gut tells me to approach with caution." She turned her attention to the trees where they had just been. Dakota leaned close to her, also watching.

Light flashed in the middle of the trees. The surge of illumination was so quick she almost thought she'd imagined it.

"I saw it too," said Dakota.

The forest grew in a half circle around the cove. They both stood very still. The light appeared again, this time at the edge of the forest. It swept over the shore toward the boat in an arc and then disappeared.

She let out a heavy breath. "That could be the man

who started the fire. Maybe he found a flashlight in that shed."

"Could be," said Dakota. "And it could be the people connected to that boat coming out to check on it."

"I suppose we need to find out who we're dealing with," she said.

They made their way toward the center of the forest where they'd seen the light. Stepping slowly and silently, they moved deeper into the trees, farther away from shore. The crash of the waves faded. Still they did not see the source of the light or any sign of other human beings.

Grace's feet padded softly on the moss of the forest floor. She sought cover behind the trunk of a tree. She signaled Dakota to stop. Faint and barely discernible above the wind and creaking branches, human voices seemed to murmur.

The sound was once again drowned out by the wind. With Dakota close behind her, she moved in the general direction the voices had come from.

They walked for several minutes before she heard people talking once again. This time the voices were more distinct. She could distinguish two, maybe three different voices, all male. The men would talk and then fall into silence. As they drew closer, the voices grew louder and more intense. The men were arguing.

She moved from tree to tree, close to the voices, until she had a partial view of the men. Dakota moved forward slowly as well, hiding behind trees and peering out. The men's foul language and rage did not suggest friendliness. All the men had on rain gear and they had built a small fire.

One of the men had a long blond ponytail. He shoved

the other. "How much longer are we going to hold up here? The storm is dying down."

The man he shoved, muscular and wearing a baseball hat, pushed on Ponytail's shoulder and then leaned close to his face. "I'm not piloting that boat out in those waters. Moving that cargo is not worth my life and losing that cargo is not an option."

"In another couple of hours this place will be crawling with Coast Guard and other search and rescue. They will have people in the air. I don't want to get caught with that cargo," said Ponytail.

Grace wondered if the *cargo* referred to drugs.

A third man sat on a log, warming himself by the fire, not talking. The dinghy boat was behind him.

Grace's breath caught when Joe stepped into the clearing. Two men drew a gun on him. Joe raised his hands. "Hey, whoa, I'm on your side."

"Search for a gun," said Ponytail.

The muscular man stepped forward and patted down Joe. "How'd you end up on the island?"

"My boat capsized. Give me a ride and I can help you get your cargo where you need to transport it. I have connections. Officials that will look the other way. I need your help with something."

A chill trickled down her spine. The *something* Joe was referring to was probably about killing her and Dakota.

"I don't think you understand the nature of our cargo," said the muscular man.

Dakota lifted his chin to get Grace's attention. He pointed back through the trees. Dakota slipped deeper into the forest and she followed. Her bare foot scraped a sharp object. She lifted her foot and stumbled but caught herself. Her other foot landed on a branch, breaking it.

Behind her, she heard voices.

"What was that noise?" one of the men said.

"There are two other people on this island," said Joe. "And they are not your friends."

"Better check it out."

She wasn't sure who had spoken. All she knew was that she needed to get away and fast. Heart racing, she sprinted over the uneven terrain. She caught glimpses of Dakota up ahead through the trees. He ran faster than she did.

Behind her, the men shouted as they crashed through the forest after her. She lost sight of Dakota. Her feet were scratched and cut. She ran even faster as the noise of the men pursuing her grew louder. A gunshot filled the air. Loud enough to be heard above the wind. Close enough to cause reverberation on her eardrums.

Panic filled her. She kept running, searching the forest for Dakota.

Hands grabbed her, yanking her off the path and deeper into the trees. She struggled for a breath as a hand went over her mouth.

FOUR

Dakota took his hand off Grace's mouth. Once she figured out it was him who had grabbed her, he knew she wouldn't scream.

"We can't outrun them. We have to outsmart them," he whispered.

Judging from the voices, at least two men were searching the forest and they had guns. He grabbed Grace's hand and hurried back up an incline that would take them closer to the clearing where the men had the fire. The men would not be looking for them to move toward the little camp. Pulling Grace along with him, he slipped behind a moss-covered log. A second later, footsteps pounded past them. He crouched below the log, bent over so his chin touched his knees. The top of Grace's head brushed against the top of his. Neither of them moved. He heard another man walking close to where they were. The footfalls were slow and even.

Dakota held his breath.

The footsteps seemed to fade. Dakota lifted his head. Two men were conferring in muffled tones some distance away.

Grace brought her head up and stared into his eyes,

waiting for his signal. He lifted his eyebrows to let her know it was time to run. He bolted upright. This time he made a beeline for the shore, pushing hard and fast through the thick of the trees.

Though the waters were still choppy, getting on that boat and escaping was their best chance for staying alive. He glanced over his shoulder. Grace was a few feet behind him. He ran faster.

Grace screamed but it sounded like the scream had been chopped in half. Joe had Grace in a tight hold, one arm around her waist and the other over her mouth.

Joe shouted, "I got her, guys." He looked right at Dakota. "And of course, you won't leave without her, so I have you both."

Fueled by rage, Dakota lunged toward Joe. Grace kicked Joe hard in the shin. Joe didn't loosen his grip, but the move gave Dakota time to raise his hand and land a blow to Joe's jaw.

He could hear the other men coming closer. They didn't have much time.

He hit Joe again. Grace elbowed him in the stomach. Joe let go. Dakota hit him one more time. This time the man crumpled to the ground. Grace had already taken off running. He could hear the men close behind them as they darted through the trees.

Another shot was fired. Seeking cover, Grace zig-zagged to where the trees grew close together. Dakota followed. They made their way toward the shore with the men close behind them. Their feet touched the rocky shore and then the sand.

Grace lunged into the waters of the cove and he dove in behind her. He was trained to swim in turbulent water, but she wasn't. He caught up with her.

The men had reached the shore. Only one of them dove in after him and Grace.

Grace was losing the battle in fighting the waves. The muscular man who had come after them seemed to be struggling as well.

Dakota grabbed Grace around the waist and swam with her for a few minutes. They were only feet from the boat. He swam ahead, boarded the boat and tossed the life preserver to her then pulled her in.

Both of them were breathless and soaked to the bone. The wind seemed to cut right through him. The muscular man treaded water and bobbed, probably trying to regain his strength. The second man, the one with the blond ponytail, stood on the shore holding his gun.

Dakota raced to the control panel and pressed the button that would lift the anchor. He was grateful to see the key had been left in the ignition. He switched on the engine. Gears turned and the motor roared to life.

The man in the water swam toward the boat. Grace paced the deck, probably looking for something to fight him off with. The boat rocked and swayed. Grace fell to one side, reaching out to the railing for support.

The man had reached the boat. He held on to the ropes on the side of the boat, trying to climb on. Even in the cove the water was rough and the waves intense.

Dakota hoped he hadn't made a mistake in trying to escape this way.

He edged the boat forward.

When he looked back the man had let go of the ropes and was swimming back to shore. Joe and the man who had been sitting by the fire emerged through the trees carrying the dinghy.

Their boat left the cove and entered open water.

Waves battered the sides of the craft. Water spilled over the deck. The hull of the boat creaked from the impact. Grace clung to the railing.

"Get belowdecks," Dakota shouted at Grace.

"But you'll be out here alone."

"Grace, please."

Another wave loomed toward them, towering above the boat like a monster, and then crashed over the deck. Grace made her way to the ladder that led belowdecks, still clinging to the railing until she had to let go to access the ladder.

He watched her disappear. He steered the boat farther away from the island. Waves continued to batter it. One wave hit him like a brick wall. He lost his grip on the steering wheel as the wave carried him across the deck. The force of the water flung him over the side of the boat where there was no railing. He grabbed the rope and pulled himself back up.

Going out into open water was a mistake. He steered back toward the island, looking for a place to drop anchor that would be far enough away from the cove where the men were. Without the dinghy, he and Grace would have to swim ashore or take their chances and stay in the boat.

He prayed for safe harbor until the storm broke all together and that help would find them. He prayed too that the men would not figure out that they'd returned to the island and come for him and Grace.

Once she got to the bottom of the ladder, Grace saw that the cargo the men referred to was not drugs. The lower deck was lined with cages filled with birds and reptiles. All of them probably illegal to bring into the

United States. Each time another wave hit the boat, the birds fluttered and cried. The reptiles seemed less disturbed by the rockiness of their ride.

As the boat pitched from side to side, she searched for a place to sit. The cargo took up most of the space. A small room at the stern of the boat seemed to serve as sleeping and eating quarters. There was only a bunk bed, a small refrigerator and a coffee maker bolted to the counter. A small propane heater was in a corner. The men must have rested in shifts.

She sat on the lower bunk listening to the water slosh around the hull of the boat. She opened the refrigerator, which contained beer and oranges and some wheat-looking substance that might have been some kind of specialty food for one of the animals. The craft's motion made her nauseous. Though she was starving, she wasn't sure she'd be able to keep anything down.

She searched in the storage compartments for dry clothes and located a pair of men's jeans and a sweater. Both of them were clean but a little big on her. She found pants and a shirt for Dakota as well.

After about twenty minutes, the boat's engine stopped humming. She could hear the anchor being lowered. Though the boat was still battered by the waves, Dakota seemed to have located calmer water. He must have decided that the journey out into open water was too treacherous. That meant Joe and his new associates might find them. They hadn't gone that far.

The stairs creaked as Dakota made his way down the ladder. She peered out through the doorless back room.

Dakota stared at the cages of animals. "Wow."

"Yeah, it's not what I would have thought either," she said.

Dakota rubbed his stomach. "Is there any food?"

She'd noticed some canned goods in her search for clothing and the oranges looked edible. "Yes, and I got you some dry clothes."

"Thanks." He stepped toward her and she handed him the clothes.

She went into the room with the animals so he could change in the cramped living quarters.

Dakota continued to talk while he changed. "We anchored close to the island. If the men go to a high spot, they will be able to see where we are."

"I'm sure they're not happy about us taking their cargo," she said.

"We're going to have to keep watch." He stuck his head out fully dressed. "Feel like eating something?"

She rested her palm on her stomach. "I can try."

He sat down on the lower bunk and she sat beside him while he peeled an orange.

"There's cans of tuna in that cupboard. I'll open one up." She located a can opener and two forks before sitting beside Dakota.

Dakota handed her a wedge of orange. She bit into it. To her surprise, it tasted good.

They sat side by side, their shoulders touching.

They finished the tuna, each of them taking turns scooping up a bite. Grace remembered the meals they used to eat together as husband and wife, looking at each other from across the table or sitting in lawn chairs in the backyard. That life, the one they'd had together, felt like it had just ended yesterday.

"That hit the spot," he said.

She nodded. His shoulder pressed against hers. The

flood of memories was like a sword slicing through her heart.

They sat for a moment in silence.

"Do you want to take first watch or should I?" Her voice faltered as she remembered the pain they had caused each other when their marriage ended.

His hand covered hers. "You okay?"

The warmth of his touch seeped through her skin. How could she tell him that being close to him reopened old wounds? "It's just everything, Dakota." Had she been running away for three years, taking assignments in foreign countries, dangerous assignments, all to forget how her storybook life had fallen to pieces?

"Everything?" He turned to face her, scooting away.

She stared into his deep brown eyes. She didn't know where to start or how. Truth be told, she wasn't sure she was ready to visit the past. The boat pitched. She fell forward against his chest. He wrapped his arms around her.

"It's going to be okay," he whispered in her ear. "I'll get us out of this." He pulled away. "I hope that hug didn't upset you."

She smoothed over her hair with her hand. "No, it's okay. We were married once. We slept in the same bed, shared meals and…" Her voice trailed off. She couldn't bring herself to talk about Anita. Feeling a rush of sorrow, she jerked to her feet.

"Has there been anyone in your life in the last three years?" He rose to his feet as well.

"No. How about you?"

He shook his head. "Work keeps me busy."

"Yeah, me too." She could feel herself retreat emotionally. This was not a conversation she wanted to have. It was easier to focus on their immediate circumstances. "A boat like this should have some flares. We could shoot some off so the Coast Guard can find us."

Dakota shook his head. "We might just let the smugglers know where we are too."

Fear stabbed at her heart. They were not safe yet. "We should probably keep watch so those guys don't come after us."

"I'll go first. Why don't you get some rest? I can't stay up there the whole time. It's too stormy and wet. I'll just check above deck every twenty minutes or so. You should do the same when it's your turn."

Dakota retreated to the cargo room. She could hear the ladder creak as he climbed. She took the lower bunk, closed her eyes and tried to sleep.

After a few minutes, she heard Dakota in the next room talking softly to the caged animals. He always did have a big heart.

She rested but never really fell into a deep sleep. When she heard Dakota climbing the ladder and then returning belowdecks, she sat up in the bunk. After wrapping the blanket around her, she rose and stood at the door with her arms crossed.

Dakota was making cooing sounds at one of the birds. "These poor guys. They have no idea why they are being put through this."

She stepped across the threshold and stood beside a cage that contained a white cockatoo. "Yeah, I suppose they will need to be kept as evidence."

"You get any sleep?"

"I tried," she said. "I got some sleep back at the light-house."

"I remember you're the one who couldn't sleep on boats or planes."

She laughed and then gave him a friendly punch in the shoulder. "Yeah, but you could fall asleep at the drop of a hat."

He pounded his chest. "Yup, that's my superpower."

They both laughed. Dakota had been her first and only love. They'd met while training to be agents. She could not just wash away the six years they had had together.

"We had some good times," she said.

"That's for sure." His gaze rested on her for a long moment.

Again, she could feel the walls go up around her heart. "I'll keep watch. Why don't you try to rest?"

He disappeared into the little room. She found a corner that wasn't occupied by a cage and rested her eyes for a few minutes before going up the ladder.

She stuck her head above the deck, which was awash with water. Dark rolling waves surrounded the boat. Dakota had piloted the boat inland where trees close to the shore provided a degree of protection from the wind. The sky was still dark and foreboding, though the rain, lightning and thunder had stopped. She turned a half circle, looking for any sign that the storm might finally be breaking up. In the distance, the rain came down in gray sheets and all around the clouds were dark with only a small clear patch of blue.

She studied the shoreline, not seeing anyone. Off to the east, she saw smoke rising up. That was probably the lighthouse still burning. They really hadn't gone far from the cove where they'd left the four men. If the Coast Guard was anywhere close, they would have seen the fire.

She crawled back belowdecks, wrapping the blanket tighter around her to warm up. She rested her head against the wall. Despite the restlessness of the birds, she fell asleep.

She woke with a jerk.

Dakota was standing in front of her. He was wearing a pair of rubber boots. The boat was not rocking as much.

"I think we got a chance to get out of here. Look around for some shoes. And meet me above deck."

Grace opened and closed storage areas and found a pair of canvas deck shoes that were at least a size too big, but they would have to do. After stuffing some paper in the toes, she slipped into the shoes and tied them as tight as she could. She still felt like her feet were swimming in them.

She could hear Dakota trying to start the engine. Though it sputtered, it never sparked to life. She crawled above deck.

"We got company," said Dakota.

She looked toward the edge of the cove. Joe and the man who had been sitting by the fire waited on the shore. Her gaze fell between the shore and their boat where the other two men rowed the dinghy toward them. Both the muscular man and the one with the blond ponytail wore visible shoulder holsters.

Pushing down the rising panic, she scanned the deck

for some sort of weapon. There had to be a way to stop or delay them so they could escape. If they could escape.

"Why won't it start?"

"I'm not sure. I've got some spark. But it only makes a grinding noise."

Dakota pushed the starter button again. The engine sputtered and died.

A sense of dread filled her as the men with guns drew closer.

Dakota peered over his shoulder. Even though the two men had to row the dinghy by hand, they were within ten yards of the boat. He glanced at the control panel.

Grace picked up a roller speargun, a sort of sophisticated harpoon with a gun-like trigger on the end used to catch fish; because the spear was attached to cording it could be reeled back in. "Did you see anything that would start a fire?" She pointed at the speargun. "This would be a bigger deterrent if it was on fire."

"There was a propane heater in the living quarters so there must be a lighter or something."

Grace disappeared belowdecks. Dakota grabbed the flare gun. At best it would serve as only a distraction until Grace could get her flaming arrow together. Would it have been smarter just to shoot the speargun? The dinghy was not inflatable. The arrow wouldn't puncture it and make it sink. The fire would only slow them down. The two men continued to row.

Dakota aimed the flare gun so it would fall into the dinghy. Both men stopped rowing. The muscular man took off his coat and wrapped the hot flare up and tossed it overboard. He shook out his coat. Dakota shot another flare toward the boat. In another five yards the men would be close enough to shoot at him.

Even as he aimed the flare gun, his mind was trying to figure out why the engine wouldn't start. The boat had sounded fine until they entered the cove and he'd tried to start it again. He stared down into the murky waters, which were thick with plant life. Something must have tangled in the rotor underneath the boat.

Grace emerged from belowdecks holding rags and a lighter. She wound a piece of clothing around the arrow then set it on fire, lined it up on the dinghy and pulled the trigger. The man let go of his oars, and both of them rose to their feet and began stomping out the fire while she pulled the speargun cable back toward their boat.

"I've got to clear the rotor." Dakota squeezed her shoulder.

"What?"

He pointed at the speargun. "Keep up the good work."

Before she had time to argue with him, he dove into the chilling waters. His hands sliced through the water. He reached out and felt along the hull of the boat until he was at the back. He dove under, feeling for the rotor. Sure enough, there was a tangle of plant life stalling out the boat.

He pulled out some of the reeds then bobbed to the surface to grab a breath of air. The two men were still stomping the bottom of the boat. Grace must have shot another flaming arrow. One of them spotted Dakota, pulled his gun and aimed. Dakota ducked beneath the surface of the water as the bullet zinged through the water. He cleared more plant life around the rotor. His fear was that even if they could get the boat going, the rotor might just pick up more plant life and stall them out.

He swam to the starboard side of the boat and shouted up at Grace. "Start the engine and go hard and fast." Maybe if they got up enough speed quickly, they could escape without getting tangled in the reeds.

Grace peered over the edge of the boat. "Got it."

She knew enough not to argue with him or ask for an explanation. When they had worked together as agents, the trust they had for each other had often kept them alive.

The men had put out the fire in their boat. Fueled by rage, they seemed to be rowing faster than ever.

The engine started up and the boat surged forward. Dakota grabbed hold of the side ropes, preparing to climb aboard. Gunshots zinged around him. He dove underwater, forcing him to let go of the rope. The boat was getting away from him.

He swam underwater until he had to come up for air. Grace stood on the port side of the boat, tossing out a life preserver. The men were rowing again to get back into shooting range of the boat. The boat continued to surge through the water. Grace must have switched to cruise control. She needed to get back at the helm if they were to get up any speed and get out of the cove. He swam toward the flotation device, grabbed hold and let the boat drag him along.

The men in the dinghy continued to row but grew farther away.

Once they were out in open water, Grace slowed the boat and towed the life preserver in. For the last few yards, Dakota let go of it and swam to the side of the boat. Grace reached down and pulled him up on deck.

Exhausted and cold, he rested on his belly for a moment while the water dripped off him. "That was a close one. Thank you for your fast thinking."

Her hand touched his shoulder. "You're shivering. I'll man the boat a little while longer until I'm sure those guys aren't going to follow us. You go down below and get warmed up." Her voice held such deep tenderness it brought back feelings he thought were long dead. The character quality he'd loved the most about her was her kindness.

He slipped belowdecks and walked past the caged animals into the tiny living quarters. He started the propane heater and searched around for more dry clothes. Once changed, he wrapped himself in a blanket and sat close to the heater.

The boat engine hummed along through much calmer waters. He had just stopped shivering when Grace popped her head in. "Good news—we've been spotted by a Coast Guard rescue boat. They're coming toward us."

He looked up at her. Her expression glowing. Her brown hair in waves around her face. "I guess that's it then. End of the line for us."

"Yes. We still work good together, don't we?"

He nodded as an intense pain squeezed his chest tight. He didn't like the idea of saying goodbye to her. "Yeah, we always did."

"The Coast Guard will be here in a few minutes. They'll want to take this boat in and figure out who has jurisdiction over the illegal cargo. I'm sure they will want statements from us and descriptions of the men.

Hopefully, they'll be able to nab them before they get off that island." Grace was back to thinking like a DEA agent. All business.

Maybe for her the chasm between them was still too wide to cross. He couldn't sort through his own feelings. He hadn't expected to ever see her again once the divorce was final. But now that they would go their separate ways, he felt an ache inside he didn't quite understand.

FIVE

Twenty minutes after they boarded the Coast Guard boat, Grace was belowdecks in clean dry clothes and holding a steaming cup of coffee. One of the Coast Guard members had taken over the boat with the smuggled animals to bring it in to shore.

Grace had explained the situation to the Coast Guard captain about the men on the island. He had assured her he'd notify the proper authorities. The smuggling was not for DEA to handle. But making sure Joe got picked up was.

She could hear the men and one woman above deck chatting and laughing. The storm had let up even more. Dakota's voice was distinct even through the sound barrier of the ceiling. The noises above her died down. The stairs creaked and she saw a pair of feet. Dakota appeared. "Good news. That rescue chopper I was on made it back to base." He walked over to the counter and poured himself a cup of coffee. "The guys said they spotted the fire at the lighthouse. It took them a while to get here because of all the other rescues going on."

He had changed into dry clothes as well. They were a bit ill-fitting. The T-shirt he had on was tight through the chest while she all but swam in the sweatshirt she'd been given.

He took a seat opposite her at the table.

An awkward tension seemed to be materializing between them. What did they say to each other now that they were safe? She wondered too why he hadn't just stayed on deck with his compatriots. It was clear they all had a positive connection with each other. Hours of training and life-and-death situations tended to do that. She'd felt a separateness from the other agents ever since she'd returned to work. Though it hadn't always been that way. Being undercover meant you could never show your true self to anyone. It was a way of hiding from the world, not having genuine connection with people.

Dakota stared into his coffee cup and then turned it in a half circle. He cleared his throat.

"You don't have to be down here with me, Dakota. It sounded like you were enjoying the conversation on deck."

"No, I wanted to come down here and be with you." His gaze landed on her and then back on the table. "After the divorce, I didn't think I would ever see you again."

They had friends in common. She had heard about him from time to time. But really, the injury they had caused each other ran so deep, they had both probably put deliberate effort into making sure they didn't cross paths.

"I know we both work out of Seattle, but it's a big city. I didn't think I'd ever see you again either." She shifted in her seat, feeling the discomfort intensify. What was he intending?

"You look good, Grace." Light seemed to flash in his eyes when he looked at her.

She touched her hair self-consciously. "That's how things work out when the ocean is your beautician."

His mouth turned up into a smile. In that moment, she saw some of the Dakota she had fallen in love with.

"Same old Grace, still wisecracking." He sat back in his chair. "You never could take a compliment."

She studied him for a long moment. Some of the tension between them seemed to have dissipated. "Maybe that's true." It was her turn to stare at the table. "I'm glad it was you that jumped into that ocean to rescue me." She wanted to tell him about the crying out to God when she thought she was going to die, but she wasn't sure if he would understand. Neither of them had professed any kind of belief or curiosity about God when they had been married. She also didn't want to destroy the warmth of the moment between them.

Again, he cleared his throat. "So you were on some kind of undercover assignment?"

She sat up a little straighter in her chair. Whatever ember had sparked between them had lost its golden glow. She saw now that he'd come down here with an agenda to ask her about work and maybe tell her not to take dangerous assignments again. She found herself becoming defensive. "Like I said before, I can't talk about it."

He shifted in his seat and then clutched the coffee cup. "You don't have to. It's just that I worry about you. With undercover work you're so alone in the fight and the possibility of—"

"You don't need to worry about me anymore," she

interrupted "We're not married, remember?" The intensity of her words surprised her.

Whatever bridge had been built between them was quickly dismantled. All the pain of the past seemed to be rushing at her at a hundred miles an hour. He hadn't been there for her when she'd needed him the most after they'd lost Anita. His deciding to care now felt like a case of too little, too late. It was as if all the sorrow over the loss and anger of how he had abandoned her three years ago was just beneath the surface. She could keep it at bay if she worked these jobs and if she didn't have to interact with the intense reminder of all the loss: Dakota.

"That guy tried to kill you, Grace."

"But he didn't kill me. My relationship with Joe is a little tainted. Though he didn't admit it outright, his actions suggest he's connected to the drug smuggling—and he's the first person I got to do that in my undercover role. He said he didn't want me as competition, which is when he first tried to get rid of me. I'm not sure how important he is in the distribution network. DEA may have to put someone else on him to watch his movements. But I am the first agent to make progress in the investigation."

"Maybe we can talk more about this some other time." His tone was a little frosty. He'd picked up on her emotional retreat even though she didn't think she'd given up any clues in her body language, a learned skill from her undercover training. Only Dakota could read her like a book no matter how practiced she was at not giving anything away.

"I don't know if there's going to be another time. We don't really run in the same circles anymore," she said.

He let out a heavy breath. "True." Dakota gulped his

coffee and then set the cup on the table. "It was good to see you."

What was that she saw in his eyes? Disappointment maybe. She still cared about him and didn't want his feelings to be hurt. She would admit to that much. "We do make a good team when we work together. We always did." If it was that easy for hurt feelings to rise to the surface just by interacting with Dakota, it probably meant they wouldn't see each other again. Maybe that was for the best.

He rose from his seat and headed back up the stairs. A moment later, she could hear him becoming a part of the conversation above deck. She rested her palm on her chest. Her stomach felt like it had been stirred with a hot poker. Something about Dakota was different. She felt drawn to him at the same time that she wanted to push him away. There was a part of her that didn't want to admit that maybe Dakota was right. She liked the work because it gave her a sense of purpose. With each drug dealer she put in jail, she knew it might give some kid who was thinking about using drugs a fighting chance at a good life. Though it often felt like she was trying to empty the ocean with a spoon, the work she did got her out of bed each day.

Still, Dakota pressing her had given her pause.

She felt comfortable in the high-risk assignments for a reason and maybe it wasn't a healthy reason.

Despite the joking and ribbing of his fellow compatriots, his brothers- and sister-in-arms, Dakota found himself disengaging from the conversation. He walked to the bow of the boat and stared out at the dark waves while the breeze ruffled his hair. Though the sky was still overcast, the worst part of the storm seemed to have passed. The boat surged up and down as it cut through the water.

It felt like a weight was resting on his chest, making it hard to get a deep breath. Seeing Grace had brought on a tsunami of emotions. Did he still love her? He couldn't say one way or another. All he knew was that there was something unresolved between them.

Grace was right. It wasn't his place to tell her how to live her life. He didn't blame her for being angry. He hadn't been there for her when she'd needed him most.

He'd give anything for a second chance to be there for her, to prove to her that he would not run out on her when she needed him.

SIX

Grace sat down in one of the chairs at the conference table in the debriefing room of the Seattle DEA. Five days had passed since she and Dakota had been taken off the boat with the illegal cargo. She'd had time to write her report and rest. She was anxious to get back to work. Though she was required to take days off, they made her restless. The downtime had given her too much opportunity to think about Dakota. His soft response to her defensiveness made her think that maybe she had been too hard on him.

Grace stared out the window at the Seattle skyline. She shifted in her chair and then laced her fingers together and rested her hands on the table. Her nerves were on edge. Her supervisor had read her report and would now make a recommendation if she could continue in her undercover role, maybe on a different ship. She was also anxious to find out if Joe had been picked up or if DEA was choosing to track him to see if he would lead them to bigger fish.

Her supervisor, Henry, entered the room holding her report, along with the woman who was her DEA contact when she was undercover. Henry Ward and Elise

Holms were both much more seasoned agents than she was. Henry had done undercover work. He understood the risk. If they thought she was in too much danger or her cover had been compromised, she'd be pulled from the assignment. Though she had a good rapport with Henry, her relationship with Elise was a little strained. Elise was only a few years older than her. Grace felt like Elise had been promoted to a supervisor position without enough field experience to really understand what the undercover agents went through.

Joe had not indicated that he was onto her as an agent. Her hope was that she could resume her role as someone trying to get in on the drug trade. Joe telling other people she wanted in would only aid her in her assignment, though she didn't care to see Joe again.

Henry and Elise smiled and selected chairs on the opposite side of the table from her.

Grace took in a breath through clenched teeth. "Just give it to me straight."

"I wish I could," said Henry. "But things have gotten complicated in the last five days."

Grace shook her head. "How so?"

"The man you identified as Joe. The one who indicated he didn't want any help from you in his trafficking operation…"

Grace nodded, feeling the tension in the room.

"One of my informants tracked him down." Elise laced her fingers together on the table. "His body was found in an alley at the waterfront by Pier 56, bullet wound to the head."

Grace took in a quick sharp breath. "So he made it to shore and someone killed him."

Elise rested her palm on her copy of the report. "Initial autopsy report indicated he'd been dead for at least three days."

Grace was still trying to piece everything together. "Were the three men who were smuggling the animals found?"

"Two of them were picked up once they were in the city. After you and Dakota were rescued, we think the men rowed to a nearby island where they were able to board a ferry. Lots of people had been stranded there because of the storm, so they blended in."

"They must have left right after we saw them," said Grace. "Once the Coast Guard picked us up. I'm sure the authorities were alerted."

"We don't think the smugglers had anything to do with Joe's death," Elise said.

"The hit on Joe was very professional," Henry added, "double taps to the forehead. After his murder, a drug shipment was confiscated at the Canadian border headed into Montana. Since the operation kept on going after his death, he wasn't the guy running it."

"So where does that leave me?" Grace's stomach tied into a knot. She dreaded what they might say.

"We want you to go back undercover, but in Montana. The man who owns the cruise line where the drugs were being transported, Mitchell Wilson, has a second home there. You're to get a job as a cook in his home."

The tightness she felt in her stomach let up a bit. She wanted to see this case to the end.

"We don't want you to go in alone," said Henry. He pressed a button on an intercom that sat on the table. "Send him in please."

The door opened and Dakota stood there.

Grace jerked in her chair. "He's not even an agent anymore."

"Henry feels that for you to go in alone is just too dangerous, Grace," Elise said. "There's also an opening at Wilson's house for a driver/personal assistant. You and Dakota will act as husband and wife."

Dakota entered the room and sat two chairs away from her.

She glared at him. "Was this your idea?"

Dakota shifted in his chair and then stared at the table. "I did call Henry just to find out how you were doing."

Henry rolled his chair a few inches away from the table. "I'd just read the report of what the two of you did out there together. It was my idea to pull Dakota back in."

Dakota lifted his head and looked her in the eyes. "He thought we would be able to pull off being a couple because we used to be married."

Grace could feel her cheeks getting hot. She didn't know if she could work in close quarters with Dakota. On the other hand, she knew what a good agent he'd been. Her encounter with Joe and being that close to death had made her feel vulnerable. Obviously, Henry thought so too. Elise didn't seem to be totally on board.

"The two men we picked up informed us that one of the animals on the boat, a pangolin, the one that looks like a scaly anteater, was set to be delivered to an address in Silver Strike, where Mitchell Wilson lives. The man who paid for the pangolin has been informed that another one was smuggled for him since news has gotten around the smuggling community that the illegal animals on that boat were taken into custody. Animal smuggling and drugs are not the same thing, but it will help build your reputation as a couple who are not above illegal activity. Criminals tend to flock to other criminals. It's a small community and might help build the connections you need."

Elise swiveled in her chair. "The most important thing is to get a read on Mitchell Wilson. Henry feels strongly that he might be behind the drug smuggling." Elise pressed her lips together.

Grace picked up on some discord between Henry and Elise. "But you don't?"

"Henry is the senior investigator here," said Elise.

"I know this is dropping a bomb on you, Grace, but we can't send you in alone." Henry got out of his chair and walked to the window. "After what happened with Joe, the risk is too high. It is your call. We can have you both in a car in two hours—a car because you can't take the pangolin on the plane. We have a suitcase with mesh so the animal can breath but will be concealed. We will have new identities in place, stellar résumés that will make you a shoo-in for the jobs with Mitchell Wilson."

Grace looked at Dakota. His eyes were bright. The soft angles of his features suggested he was not worried about her decision. "I do feel like this is being sprung on me," she said. "But I want to see this case to the end. Whoever is behind all this needs to be put away." Despite the turmoil over the past that being around Dakota brought, she knew that as an agent there was no one she trusted more.

"The two animal smugglers we picked up gave the name of their contact in Silver Strike. That should set you up with a criminal element in the area, open some doors," said Elise. She tapped a pencil on the table.

"It's settled then." Henry turned back to face them. He walked across the room and placed his knuckles on the table, leaning toward them.

"The identities we've set up for you won't show any criminal history," said Elise. "You have to be able to pass a background check in order to be in Mr. Wilson's employ. We will provide with a background file and photographs of Mr. Mitchell."

"Your first names will remain the same," said Henry. "Once you get to Silver Strike, you are no longer Grace and Dakota Young. You are Grace and Dakota Deleray and you are happily married."

A lump formed in Grace's throat. She hoped she wasn't making a mistake.

The twelve-hour drive to Silver Strike was uneventful. Once there, it took only two days for Grace and Dakota to gain employment with Mitchell Wilson.

Mrs. Cindy Wilson was substantially younger than the seventy-something Mitchell. The profile they had been given to read on Mitchell Wilson said that he had two daughters and one son from his first marriage.

The second day they were in the Wilsons' mansion Dakota waited for the opportunity to search some of the private rooms. Frequent guests and a staff meant that the house usually had someone present, but the only cleaning lady on duty today had gone home with a headache and by late afternoon everyone had left the house—Mrs. Wilson to shop and Mr. Wilson had stepped out on the golf course with a business associate who drove them himself in his own pricey vehicle. The house was part of a private club that bordered a golf course and ski hill.

Besides the staff, the only other person living in the house was Mitchell's son, Justin, who spent most of his time doing outdoor activities. But the first night Dakota and Grace had stayed in the house, Justin had thrown a party with about fifty people. They hadn't seen him since.

Once he realized the house was empty, Dakota sprinted through the house to the kitchen, where he found Grace chopping vegetables. "Hurry, I need a lookout." He had to take advantage of the empty house while he could.

Without requiring an explanation, Grace put her knife down and followed him through the ten-thousand-square-foot home. Wilson kept his office locked but it would take only a moment to pick the lock, which was an old-fashioned pin tumbler type. Though the house was new with all the modern conveniences, it had a turn-of-the-century vibe to it and was furnished with Victorian-era furniture.

Dakota opened the door and pointed toward the window that had a view of the driveway. Unless someone came in on foot, she would be able to see them driving up.

Grace stood at the window. Heart pounding, Dakota opened and closed drawers in the desk, careful to put everything back the way he'd found it. Nothing seemed out of place. Wilson had a laptop that he was protective of and that wasn't in the office. He'd mentioned that he wasn't crazy about computers and preferred to do business the old-fashioned way, so it seemed odd that he would guard the laptop so closely.

Grace hurried out to check the hallway and then returned to the window. "Find anything?"

Dakota examined a spreadsheet that he'd found in a bottom drawer. "Not really. This all fits with what we know about the businesses he owns." What Dakota was looking for more than anything was signs of financial trouble, something that might have motivated Wilson to get into the drug trade to maintain the lifestyle he was used to.

"He's back." Grace whirled away from the window.

"What?" His heart pounded.

"Wilson and his golf buddy are back." She raced toward the door. "I'll try to delay them from coming upstairs."

Dakota continued to look through the papers in a lower drawer. He might not get another chance to do this.

"Dakota…hurry."

"I know, give me a second."

She was already out the door. He heard voices as the two men entered. He did a quick survey of the room before slipping out and making sure the door was locked behind him. His heart was racing by the time he stepped out into the hallway.

Voices drifted up from the kitchen. Grace must have made it down in time. He took the back stairway and circled through the house, so it would appear that he was coming out of the room he and Grace had been given as their living quarters.

Wilson's gaze landed on Dakota as he emerged from a side entrance to the kitchen.

Dakota feigned surprise. "Golf game get called off?"

Despite his age, Mitchell Wilson was a lean, muscular man in good health. His golf partner was pale and short with a widow's peak and nervous gaze. "Thunderstorm moving in. Didn't want to be out on one of the far holes when the lightning started up."

Grace took a chicken from the refrigerator. "I was just telling Mr. Wilson about tonight's dinner. My version of chicken Parmesan, roasted veggies and garlic mashed potatoes." Though her voice was steady, Dakota noticed that her fingers were vibrating as she prepared the chicken.

"Enjoying your afternoon off, Dakota?" Mr. Wilson's gaze rested long enough on Dakota to make him feel uncomfortable. "Getting settled in okay?"

Though Dakota didn't think he'd given away anything, he knew that Mr. Wilson hadn't amassed his fortune by being stupid. The man probably knew how to read people as masterfully as he and Grace could.

"Yes, but I'm ready as soon as you need me." Dakota stepped toward Grace, wrapping his arm around her back and squeezing her shoulder. "I think we are going to enjoy life in Big Sky country." Grace stiffened beneath his touch. Just a small reminder that all of this was an act. She would play her part and so would he.

Mr. Wilson and his guest excused themselves. "We'll be in the billiard room. Let my wife know when she gets back." He tipped an imaginary hat to Grace. "Looking forward to that dinner."

Dakota listened to the retreating footsteps and mumbled conversation. He offered Grace only raised eyebrows to indicate his relief. His heart was still pounding. He had loved the excitement of undercover work. If he was honest with himself, he'd admit to missing it a little.

He watched as Grace seasoned the chicken.

"I always did like your cooking, Grace."

"Thank you." She smiled but it didn't quite reach her

eyes. "The Wilsons seem to like it so far. That's what matters, right?"

Her phone buzzed. She picked it up off the counter and clicked through. "A text. It's in code, but it looks like our contact that the arrested smugglers gave up has set a time and place to drop off the pangolin at 3:00 a.m. He wants me to come alone."

"Of course, you are not going alone. It just means I stay in the shadows." His stomach twisted into a knot. "Looks like we're not getting much sleep tonight."

In their room, Grace slept with only the top blanket on her. Her sleep was light and restless. In only a couple of hours, they would need to sneak out and deliver the pangolin to the man the smugglers had ratted out.

Dakota slept on the couch. Their first night they'd both had an awkward moment until they agreed that no one was likely to know they weren't sleeping in the same bed. Their living quarters were spacious with a bathroom and private entrance.

Dakota snored, a soft rhythmic noise. Nothing annoying. She fell back asleep listening to a sound that had at one time been a comfort to her.

After sleeping for a while longer, she woke up, rolled over on her side and checked the clock. Ten more minutes before they snuck out to make contact with the pickup for the pangolin. The house had been quiet for at least two hours.

She pulled the blanket up to her chin and stared at the pattern of shadows on the ceiling. Tonight had the potential to be dangerous. She'd prayed before when her life hung in the balance and God had answered her prayer. Yet, praying still felt awkward. What did she say?

Hey, it's me?

Dakota stirred but did not wake. Nearly getting caught that afternoon had been exhilarating and scary at the same time. It wasn't that she missed working with a partner, it was that she missed working with Dakota as her partner.

She sat up in bed and pulled the covers back, turned off the alarm on her phone before it rang and got out of bed. She shook Dakota's shoulder.

"Come on, we have to go."

Dakota was awake and alert within seconds. Both of them were fully dressed.

Dakota retrieved their guns with shoulder holsters from the hiding place at the back of the closet. Hopefully, things would go smoothly tonight but they had to be prepared for anything. Her heart fluttered as she clicked into the shoulder holster, feeling the weight of the pistol. She slipped into her jacket and waited by the door for Dakota. The pangolin had been kept in a suitcase that had hidden mesh so it could breathe. They had taken the animal outside at night and in the early morning so it wouldn't be seen.

The tricky part about sneaking out was that there were cameras mounted on corners of the house. The moment they had moved in they had assessed the level of security. There was no security guard watching monitors. They weren't sure if anyone even reviewed the video unless there was suspicious activity. All the same, they would have to stay out of the line of sight. Both of them had already been given the codes to enter the house.

Pressing close to the side of the house, they hurried outside then down the hill across the golf course. Houses and condos for the private club were situated around the golf course and ski hill. Walking was the better choice since driving might wake up someone in the house.

The cool night air brushed over Grace's skin. Though it was May, she was grateful she'd worn a jacket. The high elevation meant much cooler temperatures. They ran toward Silver Strike, where many of the people employed by the club members lived. Because of the nearby public ski hill and fishing and hiking opportunities, the town was set up to cater to tourists with an abundance of hotels and condos for rent. At this hour, the only sign of activity was a bar with a restaurant that advertised it stayed open twenty-four hours.

As they walked past, country music spilled out onto the street and the aroma of barbecue and fried food was heady even at three in the morning. Dakota checked his phone where Grace had forwarded to him the location where they were to meet their contact. They turned the corner and hurried up the street several blocks. The farther they got away from Main Street, the more rundown the houses looked. This must have been the old part of town. They passed a house with boarded-up windows and then several vacant lots. They came to a garage that looked like it was either not used or underused. A car without wheels sat up on blocks by the sliding garage doors. A faded metal sign indicated the place had belonged to Leland and Son Towing and Repair.

A creaking noise put Grace on high alert. She lifted her chin, tuning in to all the sounds around her.

Dakota placed a calming hand on her back. "We're

supposed to wait inside. He'll come to us," he whispered.

They tried the door, but it was locked. They circled the building until they found a place where the metal had been torn back from the framing and slipped inside. The floor was dirt. Grace waited for her eyes to adjust to the light. Tools hung on the wall. She noticed a motor on blocks on the floor. She set the suitcase that had the pangolin in it down and opened it to check on the animal. Poor guy. She'd had time to read up on the scaly anteater. Though it looked like a reptile, it was a mammal imported from China.

She walked over and placed her hand on the suitcase. "Hey, remember me?" She addressed her next remark to Dakota. "I wish there was a way this little guy could be back in his home, his real home."

He walked over to her and stood beside her. "Me too." He touched his shoulder where his gun was. "The contact should be here soon."

"Let's hope this is fruitful…and doesn't go sideways." She tensed and touched the gun hidden beneath her jacket. "I don't know what makes people get into the exotic-animal trade."

Dakota shrugged. "They have money to spend. They want something nobody else has."

They waited in the dark, each of them taking turns checking outside, walking the perimeter of the building. Laughter floated up the street. At least four or five people were headed their way. Grace slipped back inside the building before being spotted. Dakota kneeled by a dusty window that faced the street, peering just above the rim. He'd drawn his gun.

She moved in beside him. The voices came closer.

A voice rose up from outside the building. "Hey, look at this. A piece of Silver Strike history," said a male voice. The door on the other side of the building rattled.

"Leave it," said a female voice. "I want to get home. I'm tired."

"I remember when this guy had a booming business. Good old Leland," said the first voice. "All things must change."

Several other people made comments that weren't discernible and then the voices faded.

They waited another twenty minutes. Still tuned in to her surroundings, Grace settled down and flipped a metal milk crate over to use as a chair.

"Like old times, huh?"

"Sorry?" The warmth she heard in his voice caused her heart to flutter a little.

"How many countless hours did we spend together on surveillance and stakeouts?"

She laughed as the images connected with the memories cascaded through her mind. "In cramped and crazy places. Trying to get photos of suspects, waiting for stuff to happen. Yeah, I remember."

Her thoughts were interrupted by the sound of a car pulling up on the back side of the garage. The door on the side rattled again.

She hurried over to the door and drew her gun.

"Who is it?"

"It's me. Here for pickup," said a male voice. "I have a key. I will open the door. Did you come alone like we agreed?"

"Yes." She put her gun back in the holster and reached for the knob while Dakota slipped into a hiding place in a corner of the room behind a stack of old tires. The man eased the door open. He stood back mostly covered in shadows. She could see that his hair was very curly and fell past his shoulders. He was of medium build, but she couldn't tell much else.

"You got the package?" The voice sounded fairly young. Late teens or early twenties.

"Yeah, come on in." She needed to get a look at him.

"No, that's not part of the deal," he said.

She detected fear in his voice.

"I don't know why I agreed to this. Usually, they just leave the package and text me to pick it up. Why do I have to deal with a person anyway?"

"I guess because this time the package is alive."

"What?"

"I take it you pick up other things as well."

"Look, lady, you ask too many questions," he said. "Just give me the package." He shifted his weight from foot to foot, clearly growing more agitated. The man was wearing a T-shirt and board shorts. He might have had a gun stuffed in his waistband.

"I'm sorry I ask so many questions. It's just that I would like to get in on some of the action. You know, earn a little money on the side. That's what you do, right?"

"Just get the cargo, okay?" The man grew more irritated.

She put up her arms, palms facing him. "Okay, but the cage is heavy for me. My arms are tired from carrying it. Could you come in and help me lift it?" If the guy would come close enough, she might be able to get a better look at him.

"That was not part of the deal."

"Suit yourself. It will take me a second to bring it

over to you then." She stepped across the dirt floor. Dakota remained crouched in the shadows with his gaze on the door. She lifted the suitcase containing the animal. It wasn't heavy but she pretended like it was, half dragging and half carrying it. She set the cage on the threshold.

The curly haired man looked down at it. "He's in there."

"To hide him. The suitcase has mesh, so he can breathe. He eats bugs, mostly termites. I take it this is the first time your package was alive?"

"Too many questions, lady." He dragged the cage through the doorway and then lifted it by bracing it against his leg.

Once the man disappeared around the corner, she hurried outside and crouched by the edge of the building. With his back to her, the man loaded the cargo into the back of his SUV. Sure enough, he had a gun in his waistband. There was just a brief moment when the man opened the driver's side door and the interior light illuminated his face that she got a clear look at him.

Sensing that someone was watching, he looked in her direction. Heart racing, she slipped behind the building, hoping she hadn't been spotted. She pressed her back against the exterior garage wall and listened as the SUV motor revved to life and the man took off. She waited until the engine noise faded all together before she rose to her feet.

Dakota hurried over to her. "That guy was really on edge," he said.

Her heart was still pounding from the excitement. "I know. Either he was on something or he was coming off something."

"It sounds like he's the resident courier and his packages are usually of a different variety."

She turned to face Dakota, who leaned close to her so they could talk in hushed tones. "I've seen him before. His hair was pulled back in a ponytail the last time I saw him. That first night we were at the house, at Justin's big party. He was one of the guests."

"Did he recognize you?"

"I'm not sure. I stayed mostly in the kitchen. They had servers to bring the food out." The party had been held in an atrium that was visible from the kitchen. "I remember looking through the window and seeing him—I noticed him because of his long curly hair in the ponytail."

"So this is the first indication that criminal activity might link back to the Wilson household," said Dakota. "Or it could mean nothing."

Grace nodded, feeling a mixture of excitement and fear. She had a gut feeling they were in the right place.

SEVEN

After only a few hours' sleep, Dakota and Grace woke up in a quiet house. They got ready and headed downstairs for much-needed coffee before their working day would start. A maid bustled through the living room carrying a vacuum cleaner. Outside, a man sat on a riding lawn mower, the sound of which drifted through the open windows in the kitchen.

As Dakota made coffee, he pondered what it meant that a courier who probably usually hauled drugs was connected to Justin Wilson.

Grace broke some eggs into a bowl to make omelets. "I'm not sure who else is even around. I guess if they make an appearance, I can get them some breakfast. When I interviewed for the job, they implied that I needed to be flexible about fixing meals."

Though he was worn-out from lack of sleep, he liked the idea of a slow morning with Grace. Today was Friday. When they'd been married, Sunday had been their morning together to have coffee in bed and read the paper. Now Sunday was his day to wake early to prepare his heart for church.

Footsteps echoed down the hallway and Mrs. Wilson

skirted through the living room and into the kitchen. She was dressed in leggings, sneakers and an exercise top. Her long golden blond hair was pulled back in a ponytail. She was a tall, slender woman who walked with the grace of a ballet dancer. "I'm headed out to a yoga class. Mr. Wilson had to take his plane out early this morning for an unexpected business meeting." She placed a piece of paper and a set of keys on the counter. "We have a cabin outside of Ennis." She tapped the piece of paper. "This is the location. We're going to be hosting some family members as well as business associates. It will take both of you to get it ready. There are some tents that need to be set up to accommodate the guests, food preparations and we'll need you to get rid of any dust that may have settled. Electricity is via a generator." She looked at Grace. "Use the credit card I gave you to buy groceries for enough meals for the long weekend for ten people. One of them is a child. No dietary restrictions for anyone but you know one of the reasons I hired you was to make sure Mr. Wilson eats healthy. He'd have fast food every day if I let him."

"Got it," said Grace. "Do you want some breakfast before you leave?"

"No, I'll grab a protein shake at the gym after my workout." Mrs. Wilson pulled a jacket out of a closet by the entrance. "There are coolers in the garage for anything you need to put on ice on the way up there." She swung the door open and walked outside.

Dakota waited until he heard Mrs. Wilson pulling out of the driveway before he spoke. "I thought being Wilson's personal assistant meant I would be actually assisting him. So far, all he's had me do is drive him around a little."

"Maybe he wants to make sure he can trust you first?" She poured the scrambled eggs into the frying pan before stepping closer to him and whispering, "You know, undercover work can take months to gather any kind of significant info. Last night was a decent start. We need to find out the name of Justin's friend. DEA can run him through the system."

She was standing close enough to him that the side of her shoulder rubbed against the side of his. Floral tones of her perfume filled the air around him. Her proximity made his heart beat faster. "I know. We could be here for months."

Grace grabbed her phone off the counter and the piece of paper Mrs. Wilson had left. "Looks like I will have to meal plan on the hoof. Let's go to the grocery store."

Several hours later, they were headed up the road that led to the cabin with a car filled with food. Dakota drove. Being in the car alone allowed them to talk openly without fear of being overheard.

From the passenger seat, Grace turned to look at him. "I know you haven't had much of a chance to interact with Mr. Wilson, but what is your impression?"

"He's wrapped up in his work. He regards his son as a disappointment. Maybe his two daughters will be at this gathering."

The cabin came into view. As he drew nearer, he saw that it looked out on a lake surrounded by evergreens. Dakota brought the car to a stop.

"I'll open the place up if you want to start unloading," said Grace as she pushed open the car door and headed up the stone walkway.

Grace disappeared inside while he opened the back

of the SUV and pulled the first cooler out. They took in several more loads before remaining inside. While Grace put away groceries, he pulled the sheets off the furniture. The place was set up to entertain without electronics. There was a billiard room and stacks of board games and books. When he peered out a back window, he saw a small boat and several kayaks stacked on the rocky shore by a wooden pier. He unlocked the back door, where he found a huge deck with a barbecue. When he checked his cell phone, there was no signal. The cabin was clearly intended as a place for people to be unplugged from technology. He needed to locate the generator.

He returned outside to retrieve the final bag of food—nonperishables. Thinking that he ought to grab the car keys out of the ignition, he opened the driver's side door. The keys were gone. Though he was certain that he had left the keys in the car, he checked his pockets.

He closed the car door and went around to the passenger's side of the car. He opened the glove box. Not wanting to raise alarm bells about who they really were, they had brought only one gun to the cabin. The gun was missing.

Grace stood on the threshold outside the cabin. "Something wrong?" She took several steps toward him.

He heard a zinging sound and then looked down as red liquid spilled out of the grocery bag. It took him only a second to realize the bag of food had been hit with a bullet. A salsa jar had been shattered.

Grace's face lit up with fear as she dove for the ground. He dropped the groceries and crawled toward her. Another rifle shot stirred up the dirt close to her head. Fear for her life raged through him like an electric jolt. He needed to get to her before the next shot was fired.

They had to find cover and fast or they would both be dead.

Pebbles dug into Grace's stomach as she crawled toward the open door of the cabin. It was only ten feet away, but it may as well have been a million miles away. They were surrounded by mountains on three sides. The shot seemed to have come from a distance. A half circle of trees closer to the cabin was a possible hiding place too.

Dakota shouted at her. "He'll line up his next shot to be at that door. Too predictable."

He wasn't wrong but trying to find another way into the cabin meant they were out in the open that much longer. Could they make it around to the back where she'd seen Dakota unlock the door? She doubted it. It was too much time out in the open.

She rolled downhill toward the side of the cabin that faced the lake. Assuming the shooter was somewhere in the surrounding mountains or trees, she'd be out of range once she was on the far side of the cabin. She pushed herself to her feet. With the corner of the cabin in view, she ran as fast as she could. Another bullet glanced off one of the logs just as she turned the corner. She pressed her back against the outside wall. There were windows on this side of the building but no doors. Because of the steep incline that led to the lake, the windows were fairly high up.

She wasn't sure where Dakota had gone until he came around the other side of the building.

"He's pretty far away, don't you think?" Her breath came in quick intense gasps.

"I think there might be more than one guy. Someone took my keys. They wanted to make sure we couldn't get away."

"Are you sure you didn't just misplace them? You were always losing things when we were married." The comment had all but tumbled out of her mouth. Here they were faced with a sniper bearing down on them, and she had made a remark about his habits as if they were a married couple on an outing to the park.

He laughed and shook his head. Maybe the laughter was to relieve tension or maybe it was over the absurdity of what she had just said. His voice grew serious again. "The gun is missing too."

"Okay, I'll guess we'll have to operate as though we're dealing with two people." She tilted her head. "Can you lift me up to that window, and I'll see if I can get it to slide open?"

He moved toward the window, cupping his hand so she could use it as a stirrup. She clasped the windowsill and reached for the frame of the window.

A popping sound pummeled her eardrums. Either there was a second man or the first shooter was closer than she had initially thought or switched positions to have access to them. Dakota let go of her. She swung from the windowsill for a second before dropping to the ground.

"I don't think we can make it to the back door. One of them has probably lined up with it, ready to shoot if we get close. Going into the house is not an option. Head down to the lake. I'm right behind you."

She darted toward the shelter of the trees that surrounded the lake. The incline was steep. Rocks tumbled down in front of her, crashing against each other. She took shelter behind a tree close enough to the lake that she could hear the lapping of the water against the shore. Dakota joined her a few seconds later. He swung around the tree to face her while she pressed her back against the trunk.

He was as out of breath as she was. "What now?"

He turned toward the lake. "Let's get in that motorboat. If he follows us, he'll have to do it in a kayak. We'll have to stay low so he can't get a shot at us."

They scrambled the remainder of the way toward the lake. When she glanced back over her shoulder, she could see only evergreens and the roof of the cabin. Even if she didn't see anyone, chances were they'd be followed.

After Dakota untied the boat from the pier, they pushed the boat away from the shore toward deeper water. Dakota pulled himself up and into the boat and then reached a hand out toward her. She crawled in. Her pant legs were soaked.

Dakota pushed the starter button. The engine sputtered but didn't catch.

Heart racing, she glanced up at the trees. No sign of the shooter.

Another shot zinged through the air. She lay flat in the boat.

Dakota did the same even as his hand reached out again for the starter button. Tiny waves pushed around the boat.

"He's moved again." She lifted her head slightly above the rim of the boat. "Where is he?"

"On the roof of the cabin," said Dakota.

It took her a moment to even see the man as he hunkered down sniper-style. He was an irregular bump on the roofline of the cabin.

"The boat isn't going to start," said Dakota.

"Maybe we can sneak back up there and try to ambush him. He's vulnerable up there."

"I think we have to assume there is a second guy who is covering him. Those shots came too fast from different places. No one repositions that quickly."

She took in a breath. On this side of the lake, if they stayed close to the shore, the trees would provide some cover. But if the shooter moved in closer, they would be an easy target from uphill.

Dakota craned his neck to look at the distant shore of the lake. Without a word, they both dove into the water. His hand touched hers briefly before they separated. With both of them surfacing at different times for air, it would be like a game of whack-a-mole for the shooter.

Grace swam underwater until she couldn't hold her breath any longer. She bobbed to the surface, took in a breath and dove back under. There was a small rock formation she aimed toward, knowing that Dakota probably had the same idea.

She reached out for the rocks, lifting only her head above water. She gasped in air and then lowered herself to eye level. The shooter was still there on the roof, as motionless as a stone. His rifle caught glints of sunlight. Dakota swam toward her from the side. She slipped behind the rocks for cover.

Water dripped off him. They were only a third of the

way across the lake. Though it was a warm spring day, the water was still cold.

"He only tried to shoot me one time. You?"

She shook her head.

"We clearly stirred something up already." Her mind was reeling. Anyone in the Wilson household and any guest that was coming up here tomorrow would know or could probably guess that they would be sent up here early.

"Do you suppose that kid figured out we work for the Wilsons and squawked?"

"He must have." Or whoever was behind this had deduced that they were DEA. She couldn't figure out how that would happen though. It was clear Mr. Wilson was still trying to establish his trust level with them, but she doubted he would be able to discover they were undercover if he was behind this. "Why come after us so quickly? We're not even networked in."

He shook his head. "Maybe that kid is more important than he let on." He cupped her shoulder. "Let's keep moving."

They dove back under. Her arms sliced through the water. She rose to the surface for a quick breath as the opposite shore drew closer. She didn't see Dakota anywhere. As she slipped beneath the water, she watched a bullet part the water in front of her inches from her head.

She swam off at an angle, arms and legs working with intensity and force despite the muscle fatigue that had set in. Her feet touched the rocky bottom of the lake though she remained underwater.

She'd have to run across a few feet of beach before she would be in the cover of the trees. For that short distance she'd be exposed, an easy target. She bolted to the surface and ran through the water. Two shots in rapid succession made her dive back down into the water. This part of the lake was only three feet deep. Her belly scraped against the rocks. She moved to the side so she would surface in a different spot. She pulled herself forward, crawling underwater as far as she could.

She burst to the surface. Her tennis shoes sunk in the sand. The trees loomed ahead. Dakota emerged from behind a tree, grabbed her and all but carried her toward the safety of the forest.

A single shot echoed at her back.

With his arm around her waist, Dakota guided her deeper into the trees. He let go of her and both of them collapsed on the ground. They were dripping wet and exhausted but alive.

Dakota rested his back against a tree and tilted his head toward the sky. "That guy has some sniper skills, huh? You think he's a pro?"

She shook her head. "I had an uncle from Montana. Hunting is big around here. A lot of guys would have that kind of skill." She gave him a friendly slap on his shoulder. "Besides, he's not that good. We're both still breathing."

He met her gaze. His smile lit up his eyes. "That we are." He tilted his head. "We can see that guy coming. If he chooses to take a kayak across the lake, we can head up shore if we have to. He'll leave once the guests show up, or maybe he is one of the guests."

"So, you're saying we wait it out. Meet the guests tomorrow as though nothing has happened and see what we can ferret out." She shifted as pine needles poked through the fabric of her pants. "It's going to look weird that I haven't done any food prep."

"Once the guests get here and it's safe to go into the cabin, I'm sure you can throw the first couple of meals together as though you've spent hours. I've seen you do it." He rose to his feet. "I'll help you."

His comment warmed her heart. "Guess I need to focus on my real job, not my pretend job."

"I get it." He sat down beside her. "We need to be convincing in both roles."

She angled around the tree so she had a view of the roof. The man was no longer there. "Do you still think there are two people?"

He shrugged. "To take my keys and then get far enough back to make those shots at a distance? It seems like a lot for one guy to do in a short amount of time."

She took in a deep breath. Judging from where the sun was in the sky, it was a little past noon. Her stomach growled. It was going to be a long twenty-four hours before guests showed up. She closed her eyes, letting the sun warm her skin, grateful for the chance to rest even if she was hungry.

Both of them startled at the sound of an engine revving to life. Grace scrambled to get closer to the shore and peer through the trees. Dakota slipped in beside her.

"Houston, we have a problem."

The man with the rifle had gotten the motorboat running and was headed across the lake.

EIGHT

Dakota bolted to his feet and reached a hand out to help Grace up. The man was already halfway across the lake. He wore a wide-brimmed fishing hat that covered most of his face. His baggy jacket made it hard to determine his age or build.

They dashed through the trees. At first, they moved away from the lake. With Grace right behind him, Dakota changed directions, moving more parallel to the lake. The body of water was a way of knowing where they were. So even though he couldn't see the shore anymore, he had to remain aware of where they were in relation to the lake. Getting hopelessly lost would put them in even more jeopardy.

They sprinted through the thick of the forest. His wet clothes slapped against his body. The terrain changed so the trees were more sparse, and they were moving uphill. A rifle shot sent them both to the ground. Adrenaline surged through him as he crawled soldier-style on the grass and dirt.

Several feet away, Grace pulled herself along on her stomach as well. The trees were too thin and too far apart to provide any level of protection.

Dakota craned his neck and scanned the landscape behind him. He looked first where he thought the shot had come from and then all around the area, not spotting the shooter. The man must have taken up a position so his shots would be more accurate. They were both dressed in bright-colored clothes that contrasted with the landscape, making them easy targets to spot.

If the man was not on the move, the only advantage they had was to put distance between the shooter and themselves. "Take turns running. You go first."

Grace nodded and burst to her feet. Dakota looked behind, waiting to see where the shot would come from. This time he saw the man holding his rifle and moving toward a rock. Grace wouldn't be shot at as long as the man was still trying to take up a position.

Grace hit the ground and he jumped up. His feet veered off at an angle. Both he and Grace switched off running, moving forward until they could take cover in a cluster of trees. He knew they had only precious seconds to catch their breath. Because the vegetation was so sparse, it wouldn't be hard to figure out where they were hiding.

He tugged on her sleeve and they kept running. They hurried up a hill and down the other side. Down below, the lake glistened in the late-afternoon sun. They took cover in the trees for several hours, watching and waiting.

Finally, they hurried down to the shore. Dakota looked back to where they had just come from, not seeing the shooter anywhere.

If they continued forward, they would have a long trek around the water. He had no idea how big the lake was. "I say we double back and get in that boat."

Grace studied him for a moment, probably assessing the risk of such a plan. "What if there is a second man waiting around for us?"

"Two against one. If we can reach the boat, the guy on this side of the lake will have to swim across to get at us. They weaken themselves by being on opposite sides of the lake."

She nodded. "Good idea. Do the unexpected." They moved silently along the shoreline and then back toward the way they had come, sometimes crouching and sometimes crawling. They took what little cover they could find in tall clumps of grass or by small rock piles. As long as they were not spotted, the smarter choice was to move slowly and keep an eye out for the shooter.

At some point, their paths would cross with the shooter's. Dakota's prayer was that they would be far enough apart to not be spotted and become a target again. If the shooter saw them and realized their plan, they'd be racing to get to the boat first.

As they traveled, the sun got lower in the sky. It must have been dinnertime by now. Neither of them had eaten since breakfast at the Wilson's house. Grace was about ten yards ahead of him crouching low, stopping often to look around but moving at a steady pace. She froze suddenly and dove to the ground.

His heartbeat revved up a notch when he hit the dirt as well. He saw the shooter stalking past them toward where they had just come from. His back was to them as he searched the landscape. Because of the color of their clothes, if the shooter looked in this direction, they'd probably be spotted. Maybe the fact that the sun was low in the sky would help conceal them.

Only partially hidden by a clump of grass, he peered

through the blades to watch. The man must have sensed Dakota's presence because he stopped, walked several feet in one direction and then stopped again.

Dakota held his breath as the man took several steps toward him. The shooter was at least ten yards away. Far enough away that Dakota could not discern facial features beneath the hat. Judging from the way the man moved, Dakota guessed he was younger, under forty. Even if he was older, he moved like a man used to physical activity.

With the rifle resting across his body and on his shoulder, the shooter turned so he was facing Dakota directly. Dakota felt like his heart had stopped beating as he willed himself to blend with the ground. The man took several steps toward Dakota. Dakota focused in on the rifle. If he moved to take aim, Dakota would have no choice but to run. The man planted his feet and turned slowly. Dakota's throat went dry. His heart pounded.

The man turned and continued to search the landscape. When the shooter had moved another twenty yards away, Dakota scrambled along the ground. He didn't see Grace anywhere. Then a flash of pink caught his eye. Grace was off to his side about ten yards away. She was still pressed flat against the earth.

He looked over his shoulder. The man's back was to them.

Now was their chance to put as much distance between them as they could. Their pace had been slow. The man had not spotted them for at least two hours. It was probably just a matter of time before he realized that they had doubled back or he turned and saw them running when they were out in the open.

If they could only get to the trees they'd be less of a target.

Both of them jogged, dove to the ground, looked over their shoulders and ran some more. They moved in a parallel pattern but never came together.

He could see the trees up ahead. When he glanced over his shoulder, he saw that the shooter had done an about-face and was stalking in their direction. Though it wasn't clear yet if they'd been spotted, the man must have realized they'd doubled back.

Dakota ran with a furious intensity and then fell to the ground. Grace was crawling on all fours, dropping to the ground and then moving again.

The first rifle shot broke the silence of the forest. It had not come near him. The shooter must have spotted Grace. She was lying on the ground facedown, her arm bent at an unnatural angle. His heart squeezed tight as he feared the worst.

Grace had plunged to the ground so quickly she now understood what the phrase *eating dirt* meant. She flicked her tongue and swiped at her mouth to clear it of the pebbles. Her arm was bent underneath her body. The bullet had come so close to hitting her that her ear-drums hurt from the sonic boom and her skin tingled as though the top layer had been scraped with a utility knife. Stillness seemed the best strategy.

"Grace?"

Dakota's panicked but soft voice came from off to the side. She dared not turn her head to look at him.

She shout-whispered back, "I'm okay."

"He's getting closer, Grace," he said. "We better run for it."

Grace lurched to her feet and sprinted into action. She pumped her legs, keeping her eyes on the evergreens up ahead. Dakota's footsteps made soft padding sounds as he sprinted too. Another rifle shot whizzed by her. She crawled for several feet. The trees were ten yards away. The shooter got off one more shot before Dakota reached the edge of the forest. The shooter had two options: to chase after her or to stop and line up a shot. She had no idea which he would choose. A rifle like that had a long range.

She was within feet of the trees when a backward glance revealed that the shooter was getting closer. The trees were five feet away. Adrenaline kicked into high gear. She leaned forward as though pressing toward a finish line. Her feet pounded the earth. She reached the edge of the forest and fell into Dakota's arms.

He'd waited for her. He gave her a quick hug. The strength of his arms around her renewed her energy. "Come on, let's hurry and get down to that boat before he catches up with us."

He veered in the general direction of the lake. She ran beside him. Behind her, she saw flashes of color that indicated the shooter was hot on their trail, but he was slowed down by carrying the rifle. Even if it had a sling and he could put it over his shoulder, the weight and bulk of it would've been a hindrance.

They moved downhill through the thick of the forest until they reached the lake. They stepped out onto the narrow strip of beach. The setting sun created marmalade-colored streaks across the smooth surface of the lake.

She didn't see the boat anywhere. They'd either overshot or undershot the location where they needed to be.

"Up this way," said Dakota.

She had to trust that Dakota was right about which direction they should go. As they ran, she glanced off to the side, seeing the roof of the cabin just above the tree line. They were headed in the right direction, but they'd be facing another assailant soon enough.

A rifle shot sent them scurrying back toward the trees. The shooter was behind them. He'd knelt to take a shot by resting the rifle on a rock.

The shoreline rounded a bend. Dakota led her back out to the beach. She could see the boat up ahead in the dimming light of evening.

They raced toward the boat and pushed it into waist-deep water. Dakota jumped in and pushed the starter button. It revved to life.

She could only guess why it hadn't started for them. Maybe it had been out of gas. Maybe there had been a loose wire.

They were a third of the way across the lake when the shooter made his appearance. He paced the shore before settling on his stomach and setting up the rifle.

They both flattened themselves against the bottom of the boat. Only Dakota's hand was exposed as he steered the boat. Her own breathing seemed to surround her as her heart thudded in her chest.

She wondered if the two men had a way of communicating with each other. Cell phones didn't work up here, but maybe they had brought radios.

The boat moved in a serpentine pattern. The man fired several shots over the top of the boat. Dakota pulled his hand away from the wheel as the boat bumped over the waves. She lifted her head. The shore was in sight.

Dakota put his hand back on the wheel. "We'll be

easy targets if we dock at the pier." He angled off to the side and then killed the engine. "It's a short swim."

She lifted her head to take in her surroundings and assess what he was suggesting. The shooter was maybe fifty yards away. The rifle probably had an accuracy range of a hundred yards in the hands of a good marksman. They could swim toward a steep embankment where the trees and brush came right up against the water. "Okay, let's go." She slipped off the side of the boat. Dakota splashed in beside her.

Kicking her legs and butterflying her arms, she swam just beneath the surface. She bobbed up to get a breath. The water became shallow enough that she could crawl and still stay under. She lifted her head so her chin remained in the water. All she had to do was reach up for the tangle of brush and pull herself through. She stretched her arm out for a branch. It broke. She fell back into the water.

A rifle shot zinged over her. The man was shooting from across the lake. Pressing close to the bank and trying to stay underwater, she moved down the shore until she found another possibility for getting on dry land.

She gripped the thin trunk of a tree, lifted and pulled and then crawled through the undergrowth. Hidden by the thick foliage, she dragged her feet up to meet her stomach. She gasped for air and waited for her heart to slow down.

Now to find Dakota.

Maybe the best option would be to head toward the house and assume that he could make it there as well. Once she was on the far side of the house or inside, the shooter wouldn't be able to get to her.

Still on high alert, she peered back through the thick

greenery. Though night was falling, she had a view of the distant shore. The shooter who had tracked them was no longer there. This concerned her. Why did it appear he was giving up? Maybe he had simply communicated with the second man to ambush them.

The boat floated lazily twenty feet from the pier. The three kayaks remained upside down on the beach. Grasshoppers sang their evening song. She didn't hear any noise indicating Dakota coming toward her.

If the second man was close by, crying out for Dakota would give away her location.

The brush and undergrowth were so thick she had to tear some of it away in order clear a path through it. She was still crawling on her belly and crouching as she headed uphill toward the cabin. Finally, the thick undergrowth ended. She still had an uphill climb.

Once she climbed halfway, she could see the back of the dark cabin where the deck and barbecue were. No lights, no sign of movement anywhere. As though a gauzy veil had been pulled across it, the sky had turned from blue to gray. The cover of night would protect her from view.

Her chest squeezed tight as she debated what to do. Make a run for the house and hope that Dakota had made it as well? Hope the second man wasn't waiting for her inside? Or hide out in the thick underbrush and hope Dakota would find her? She had never been good at staying still. Action made more sense to her.

Still crouching, she worked her way up the hill, looking for any kind of a threat. Her footsteps sounded like paper crinkling in the silence that surrounded her. She stopped to listen for human movement or voices. Nothing, though the hairs on the back of her neck were standing at attention.

She sprinted the remaining distance to the deck. All the windows inside were dark. Padding softly on the wooden deck, she reached for the back door. She gritted her teeth as it opened, and she stepped inside. She eased her way in, listening the whole time while she pressed close to the wall. She hurried past the kitchen to the living room, ducking down by a window and then peering just above it. Their car was still in the driveway. She watched for a long time, not seeing any movement anywhere. She hurried back to search the kitchen. The canned goods she'd left on the counter but not put away were undisturbed. Her stomach growled. She studied the dark kitchen, seeing no movement, no suspicious shadows.

Had Dakota had time to switch on the generator? Turning lights on would be like a beacon to anyone who wanted to do them harm, but if someone was inside, it seemed like she would at least see illumination from a flashlight or something.

Where was Dakota?

After checking that the upstairs was not occupied, she ran a patrol from window to window, searching for at least ten minutes. One of the windows in a bathroom was open. Otherwise, nothing seemed out of place.

Faint noises, which could almost be the wind rustling the trees, came from nearby. She watched the area where the sound had emanated from. An animal whose butt was higher than its head emerged, followed by three smaller critters with the same silhouette. Raccoons come to forage. A fourth baby trailed behind the others, scurrying to catch up.

She waited and watched. The clattering of metal caused her to startle. Until she realized it was the raccoons knocking over the garbage can on the other side of the cabin. Once her heartbeat returned to normal, she pressed against the wall of the bathroom. Only the muffled sounds of the raccoons consuming whatever they had found filled the air. She could not be confident that she was alone or that she wasn't being watched.

She hurried to the door, wrapped her hand around the knob and eased it open. She slipped into the hallway and pressed against the wall waiting for her eyes to adjust to the darkness.

Though she had no sensory information to verify it, her gut told her that someone else had entered the house since she'd run the first patrol. Friend or foe? Dakota or the second man? She had no way of knowing.

Her thought all along was that with Dakota's help, they might be able to ambush the second man while his partner was across the lake. Maybe they could get some information out of him and arrange for DEA to pick him up. She wasn't so sure she could do that without Dakota's help.

Her stomach growled so loudly she was afraid it would give her away. A floorboard creaked. She pressed herself tighter against the wall.

The kitchen area was open with a sort of breakfast nook next to it with a table and an angled bay window that provided a partial view of the lake and the front of the cabin. She wondered if the bay window seat was also a storage area. She hurried over and lifted the lid of the seat. The creaking noise it made caused her to cringe. It looked like it was used to store logs for the fireplace and there wasn't room in there for her. The distinct thud of footsteps reached her ears. Her heart raced. More footsteps sounded in the hallway headed toward her.

She hurried over to the kitchen table, scooted a chair out of the way and slipped under. After she had carefully dragged the chair back into place, she pulled her knees up to her chin and tucked her arms in close to her sides.

Grace remained as still as a statue as the footsteps drew closer. She watched as a man who was clearly not Dakota moved across the floor. The man stopped and turned. He clicked on a flashlight and then turned it off quickly. She watched in horror as he stepped toward the table. He had a gun in his hand.

NINE

From the back seat of the car where he'd been watching and waiting, Dakota saw a flash of light turn on and then off. When he'd come up the bank from the lake, he couldn't find Grace. Concerned that he would be a target, he'd taken refuge in the car. He'd assumed he would see Grace eventually. Now there was someone inside the house.

He'd been momentarily distracted by the arrival of a raccoon family right before seeing the light in the cabin. Dakota feared the worst. Had Grace slipped inside the cabin searching for him? She must have gone in the back way.

Furniture crashed inside the cabin, then he saw the flash of gunfire in the darkness. Panic flooded through his body as he pushed open the car door, slipped out and hurried toward the cabin.

Crouching beneath the window, he lifted his head to see what was going on. The lack of light made it hard to discern the interior of the cabin, but he saw no more movement. The place seemed to have fallen silent again. He edged toward the front door, turned the knob slowly and eased it open a few inches.

He detected the faint sound of footsteps. Someone was moving around at the other end of the house but had not turned the flashlight on again.

A tap on his shoulder made him whirl around ready for a fight. Grace wrapped her hand around his raised fist.

She put her fingers to her lips.

Though he was relieved to see her, a hundred questions raged through his mind. Inside, the footsteps grew louder. He saw a flash of light. The man was coming toward the door. Grace grabbed his hand and led him back toward the far side of the car.

They both crouched for a second.

His muscles tensed. He'd left the door open. The man would figure out they were on this side of the house. He tugged on Grace's sleeve and pointed toward the brush that grew not too far from the house. They ran toward the bushes. A light showed behind them.

The man's footsteps pounded on the outside landing.

They moved in a wide arc around the house until they were looking at the back of the house from some distance away.

"What happened in there? I saw gunfire."

"He was coming right toward me. I was hiding under the table. So I threw a saltshaker that was on the table across the room to distract him. It hit the wall and he shot at it, and when he ran over to see what it was, I bolted. Where were you?"

"Hiding in the car waiting for you to show up."

"I went in the house by the back door."

Wrapping an arm around her back and cupping her shoulder, he drew her close. "I'm just glad you're okay." He couldn't hide the emotion in his voice. "When I saw that gun flash…" He shook his head. "I just don't want to think about a world without you in it."

She didn't respond right away, and it was too dark for him to read any emotion in her expression.

"I don't regret saying that, Grace. I mean it. Maybe we weren't good together as a couple, but I still think you're a good person and the world is a better place with you in it."

She did not try to break free of the hug. "Thank you for saying that. It means a lot to me."

The power of the moment between them passed quickly as they watched the man come around the side of the house, searching with his flashlight in one hand and the gun in the other.

They retreated even farther into the woods. They were close enough to hear water lapping at the shoreline even though the trees obscured the view of the lake.

The man with the flashlight walked in a half circle around the back of the house, and then he stepped away from the house and started to search farther out. As he swung the flashlight, it came within a few feet of the area where they were hiding.

They were both on their knees, hunched over, shoulders pressed together. Dakota had the feeling Grace was holding her breath. Neither of them moved a muscle. The man swung the flashlight to the side of them, still looking. He was too close for them to risk trying to move and get away. Any sound at all would make the man swing around and shoot.

The seconds ticked by as the man methodically searched. He held the gun in his hand.

Dakota contemplated jumping him. Grace would back him up. The man was about ten feet from where they were hiding. There was too great a risk he'd hear them coming and shoot before they could overtake him.

They waited while the man slowly moved farther away. Dakota had to assume that it was just a matter of time before the guy with the rifle showed up as well. Maybe he had found a narrow place in the lake to swim across. He'd have to ditch his rifle if that was the case. There was the possibility too of other unoccupied cabins with boats. Though they had not seen any dwellings close by, it made sense that there were other lakefront properties.

The man was far enough away that they could move even deeper into the trees, which meant they were getting closer to the lake. Though the guy seemed preoccupied with searching a different area by the cabin, Dakota didn't dare let his guard down. They could talk in low voices and not risk being heard.

"I wonder if he's going to keep this up all night," said Dakota.

"One thing is for sure. We're not getting back in that house until the guests get here or those guys take off," Grace whispered. "I still think we should look for a chance to jump him before the second guy gets across the lake."

"What if these two guys are among the guests?" Dakota said. "They must have come up here in a vehicle. So there must be a spur road or someplace to park where they could have hiked to the cabin and waited for us."

"Are you saying maybe we should try to find the car?"

"It might tell us who they are even if there aren't any keys in it. At the very least once we got back to town and could make a call, DEA could run the plates so we can start figuring out who the players are here."

"These guys don't seem like amateurs to me."

"Agreed."

The sputter of a boat motor drew their attention toward the lake. They scrambled down the hill through the trees so they had a view of the pier. The shooter brought the boat to the shore, pulled his rifle out and hiked up toward the cabin as a sense of dread filled Dakota. Now there would be two armed men looking for them.

They moved in closer. Though he could not discern the words, he could hear the two men talking on the back porch and pointing at areas that surrounded the cabin. The men were putting together some sort of search plan.

"We better get out of here."

With Grace keeping pace with him, they jogged away from the lake and the cabin. The darkness slowed them down. Remembering the rocky hills where he initially thought the shooter might have been, they moved in a wide arc around the cabin, crossed the road and headed uphill. As they got up to higher ground, he could see the two flashlights bobbing in separate areas as the men searched.

Exhausted, out of breath and hungry, they took refuge on a rocky hill that provided a view of the cabin and the trees that surrounded the lake. If they slipped back toward the rocks, they were mostly hidden from view. One of the lights returned to the cabin while the other continued to search.

Dakota estimated that they had at least four more hours until daylight. Sunrise was around 6:00 a.m. The guests would start arriving around ten. Could they wait it out until the men ran the risk of being seen by the arriving guests? Once daylight came, he and Grace would be that much easier to spot.

Though they'd dried out some, Dakota's clothes were still damp from having been soaked in the lake. The evening chill made it that much colder.

"Grace, do you think you could sleep? I'll keep watch."

"I'll try."

"I know it's cold. You can rest your head on my shoulder if that helps."

"Thanks." She scooted in beside him, pressing her cheek against his shoulder. She was shivering.

"What if I wrap my arm around you? Would that help?"

"Yes," she said. She wrapped her own arm around his waist and rested her head against his chest. He drew her into a sideways hug.

He hadn't noticed the cold when they were running, but now he felt it. He watched the light bob halfway up the hill where they were perched. He tensed. The man was maybe forty yards away. As long as he didn't shine the light directly at them, they would probably just look like part of the rock formation. The man did a slow arc with the flashlight and then veered off where there were trees.

He was grateful the tense moment hadn't awakened Grace. Holding her while she slept was bittersweet. The good memories seemed to collide with all the pain and harsh words they'd shouted at each other at the end when everything fell apart. He'd meant what he said earlier. He didn't want her to risk death with the assignments she took. Even if she wasn't in his life, he wanted her to come to a place of hope like he had.

He held her and continued to watch, estimating that half an hour had passed. She stirred awake, lifting her head off his shoulder.

"Wow, I didn't think I'd be able to sleep." She stared down the incline. "He's still looking for us."

"Yes, but he didn't come this far up."

"Do you want to try to get some sleep?"

"No, I'm too wired."

They sat in silence for a long time, watching and waiting. When he'd heard the gunshot inside the cabin, he'd thought he'd lost Grace.

He rubbed his hands on his pant legs and took in a breath. "Grace, what I said back during that storm, I think it is still important to talk about. I'm worried that you take these assignments because you don't care if you live or die."

"I know you implied that when we were in the lighthouse. I got defensive because you were sort of right. I just thought I could do some good with these assignments. And I didn't have a lot to live for, but that changed in the storm when I was in the water and thought I would drown. I knew I didn't want to die."

"I went through the same thing, Grace. It's why I quit the DEA."

"You know, when I was in the water and thought I was going to die, I cried out to God." She let out a huff of air. "Isn't that funny?"

He leaned closer to her. The elation he felt created the sensation of almost floating. "No, it's not funny. Same thing happened to me just in a different way. Being with the Coast Guard guys. The work is dangerous but it's about saving people and keeping each other alive."

"DEA can be that too, but I guess I checked out in a way, isolating from the team with my assignments."

He peered off at the distant mountains to the east where a sliver of the sun rose above the rim of the mountains. "Kind of like God got a hold of both of us. Just in different ways, at different times." He reached out and placed his hand over the top of hers where it was resting on the ground.

She didn't pull away. He closed his eyes and enjoyed the moment, feeling as though something between them had been mended.

Down the other side of the rocky hill, a noise caught his attention. Both of them flipped around, resting on their stomachs and peering out. It was still too dark to see much. The noise was mechanical. The hum and roar of an engine firing up.

"That sounds like a car," Grace said.

He squinted. He could just make out what was probably a very rough road. That had to be where the men had parked to be hidden. He caught just a flash of motion as the car, still hard to discern from the surrounding landscape, took off. "That has to be them. I can't tell what make of car it is. It's almost the same color as the road, tan or gray." His gaze followed the line the men must have hiked to get to the cabin up over a hill and down the other side.

"We got a few hours before the guests show up," she said. "It's safe to go back to the cabin, you think? We should get cleaned up so no one asks questions about our appearance."

"Yeah, but we will still have to keep a lookout.

Maybe they are just planning on circling around and showing up in the car, guessing that we would head back to the cabin. Maybe one of them stayed behind."

She rose to her feet. "Let's get down there."

As the sun lifted above the rim of the distant mountains, they hiked back to the cabin. So much felt up in the air and uncertain, not just their safety for the next few hours. Even though it felt like something between him and Grace had been healed, he had no idea what it meant for their future. All he knew was that God seemed to be doing something in both their lives.

Dakota stared down the road that led to the cabin, half expecting to see a vehicle approaching or men on foot with guns. He suspected that the next few hours would be some of the longest of his life.

TEN

After they cleared the rooms and the area around the cabin to make sure both men had left, they both got changed and cleaned up. Grace worked with a furious intensity to get some meals ready. She chopped vegetables for roasting in tinfoil packets on the grill and for salad. She checked the cookies she had put in the oven. Dakota was outside setting up tents.

Dakota popped his head into the kitchen. "Still all clear. I don't think they are coming back. I got my stuff done. Do you need any help?"

Her heart lurched a little when she saw him…a very old response that she had thought was long dead. The sparkle in his eyes and the welcoming softness of his features had been what first attracted her to him so many years ago. His voice had always calmed her.

"You can chop veggies. The first meal the guests will have is tuna sandwiches with salad. A total revision of what I had in mind. We'll grill steak and veggies for dinner, so all I have to do is get some snacks done."

Dakota walked over to the counter and picked up the knife. "You're kind of in your element when you cook. I always thought that about you."

The warmth she heard in his voice made her heart flutter. She had worked as a cook all through college, never realizing how much it would benefit her in her undercover work. "Thanks, Dakota."

The sound of a car pulling up outside caused them both to stop what they were doing. She glanced at the clock on the wall. It was still half an hour before the first guest was due to arrive.

"Give me a second." Still holding the chopping knife, Dakota slipped out of the kitchen and headed to the living room.

She grabbed a knife as well and hurried to back Dakota up. Dakota stood at the big front window. "False alarm. Early arrivals."

The door swung open. Mr. Wilson's son, Justin, stepped in. From the moment she'd met him, Grace thought he looked like a surfer who had gotten lost on his way to the ocean. Deeply tanned skin and long blond hair, goofy expression.

Dakota quickly set the knife on a nearby table.

Justin stepped aside so his friends could enter. The first one who came in was also tan and in good shape but with spiky brown hair bleached at the ends.

"Sorry we're a little early," Justin said. "Looks like we got here before Dad."

"It'll be a minute until I have something for you to eat." She held up her knife. "I'm just preparing some things now."

"No problem. We'll just chill." Justin's friend was studying his surroundings in a way that indicated he'd not been here before. "This is Evan." Justin punched his friend in the shoulder.

A third man holding a cooler entered the room. His

face blanched when he saw Grace. The curly-haired kid who had picked up the pangolin. Grace knew enough to make sure her expression did not give anything away.

Justin walked over to the guy and took the cooler. "Cory, are you gettin' the flu or something?"

"I'm fine." Cory's gaze remained on Grace just long enough to make her uncomfortable.

Grace stepped toward him. "I don't believe we've met. What did you say your name was, Cory…?" She held out her hand hoping to get a last name that would allow DEA to look into him.

"Just Cory." His words held a note of hostility.

Grace addressed her comment to Dakota. "I'll be in the kitchen getting things ready." She left. The food preparation continued on autopilot. She pulled the cookies from the oven and placed the veggies in their tinfoil packets for the grill tonight. She needed to find a way to get Cory alone. Was he the reason they had been targeted to be killed?

In the next room, she could hear Dakota making small talk with the three men. Dakota had a way of disarming people. The conversation probably came across as benign while the whole time he was watching reactions and gathering information.

She sprinkled olive oil and lemon juice on the veggie packets before sealing them up and placing them in the refrigerator. She had just started to open the cans of tuna when a flurry of noise from the living room told her more guests were arriving.

From the kitchen window, she could see that Cory, Justin and Evan were headed down toward the lake. The extra boat would probably look off to them as would the boat in the middle of the lake, but the best strategy would be to claim she had no idea why it was there if they questioned her or Dakota.

"Do you have a cookie for me?" A child's voice jerked her from her thoughts.

A girl who couldn't have been more than three years old stood in the doorway to the kitchen. She had on pink tennis shoes and though she wore jeans and a T-shirt, she had a tutu around her waist.

A woman came into the kitchen and swept the child up into her arms. "I'm so sorry. Margie smelled your cookies. I'm Lynn, Mitchell Wilson's daughter."

"Good to meet you." Grace could feel herself going numb. Anita had loved to wear tutus with everything as well.

Lynn rested her forehead against Margie's. "You can have a cookie after lunch. And it looks like this nice lady is working on that right now."

"You'll have to excuse me for a minute." Without gauging Lynn's reaction, Grace hurried through the kitchen and out the back door. Her stomach churned and she thought she might be sick. The pain over the loss of Anita seemed to be coming back full force. Grief had a way of ambushing her like that even after three years.

Whatever healing had begun between her and Dakota, the immensity of the loss that could not be repaired or replaced overshadowed everything. She closed her eyes and took in a breath.

God, please help me.

At the lake down below, she could hear the three men laughing. Evan had gotten into a kayak and was paddling around. A moment later, Cory emerged through the trees, separating from the other two. She slipped a little closer to the house so he wouldn't notice her. He must have been coming back up here to use the bathroom or get something to drink.

Now was her chance to talk to him alone. There was no time to grab Dakota to back her up. She doubted he would try anything with so many people around.

Still feeling stirred up from Margie sparking a memory about Anita, she stepped out into the open and headed down the hill to talk to Cory.

Cory locked her in his gaze. He looked side to side like he was trying to figure out where to go. Then he turned and headed back toward the trees.

It would be safer if they talked out in the open, but she might not get another chance to speak with him. She followed him into the forest.

Dakota hurried through the cabin in search of Grace. Lynn and Margie had returned from the kitchen explaining that Grace had seemed upset and had run out. If the sight of the child had made him feel like an elephant was sitting on his chest, he couldn't imagine what it had done to Grace. Once he could break away from the tangle of arriving guests, he went looking for Grace. The bathroom door was open, no one in there. She would not have gone to the sleeping quarters upstairs. He stepped out onto the back deck.

Voices down the hill in the trees, one of them Grace's, alerted him to where she was. The conversation sounded heated. As he drew closer, he saw that she was talking to Cory. Dakota slipped behind a tree, ready to step in if he needed to. Part of undercover work was building trust with people who could help the investigation. He didn't want to disrupt that process.

Cory spoke up. "I don't even know who to ask to let

you in on this. I get a text. It tells me where to be and what to pick up."

"And you get paid cash? I'd really like to get in on that. Do you think Wilson pays me much of anything as a chef?"

There was a long pause before Cory spoke up. "It's not always cash. Look, I got into some trouble last winter. I like to snowboard. Meth enhanced my performance. Problem is you don't want to quit."

"Meth?"

"I'm going down to the lake to be with the guys. You need to leave this alone and you need to leave me alone. Find some other way to make money."

Dakota listened to Cory's retreating footsteps. He stepped out from behind the tree. She whirled around to face him. "Oh, it's you. Did you hear what Cory said—meth?"

"Yeah, I heard it," he said.

"It sounds like he only knows the supplier via text messages. No clear connection to the Wilson family," she said.

"We should get back up to the house. Are you okay with Margie? It kind of hit me hard."

She looked at him as pain entered her eyes and marred her features. "Yes, like a blow to the stomach. She seems like a sweet kid. I should just be able to let it go. I can't spend the rest of my life avoiding children." She ran her fingers through her hair. "Let's just do this job. I think Cory is our strongest lead."

Grace had made it clear she didn't want to talk about past pain. He couldn't blame her. They returned to the cabin. Dakota helped Grace with the food prep. More guests arrived until all ten were present, and finally, lunch was served and everyone seemed happy with the casual sandwiches, salad and fruit.

Several hours later, Mr. Wilson popped his head in the kitchen and addressed Dakota. "Skeet shooting. Could use your help with setup. You are welcome to join us if that is your thing. Just out the backyard off to the side opposite the lake."

"Got it," said Dakota. He cupped Grace's shoulder. "You going to be all right?"

"Oh, sure, there's lots of people around," she said.

He meant about being around Margie, but he decided not to press the issue. It made them both emotional. Maybe Grace was right—they should just focus on the investigation.

Mr. Wilson led Dakota to a shed where the shotguns and protective hearing and eyewear were stored. Justin and Cory grabbed shotguns along with two other men who were likely business associates of Mr. Wilson's. One of the men had the same build as the shooter who had come after them by the lake. The same ambling stride as well. Maybe it was just seeing the man with a shotgun that made Dakota think that. He and Grace had never really gotten a good look at either of the two men who had come after them. Mrs. Wilson showed up a moment later with a shotgun. Dakota helped haul the boxes of clay pigeons from the storage shed along with the ammunition.

There were four throwers for the clay pigeons set up. Dakota operated the one for Mr. Wilson. Cory, Justin and the man with the ambling stride were the first to shoot. Mrs. Wilson, Evan and a man who Dakota knew to be a business friend of Mr. Wilson's stepped in to operate the throwers.

The men alternately yelled "pull," though there was overlapping gunfire. A stray shot whizzed past Dakota when he'd stood up to stretch his legs. Dakota had been behind the safety line of fire when he stood up. He stared down at the three other shooters, who all seemed focused lining up their next shot.

"Somebody's not paying attention, huh?" said Mr. Wilson as he raised his shotgun.

"For sure," said Dakota, still studying the other three men.

They shot until the dinner bell rang. An outdoor table had been decorated and set up. Grace set the plate of grilled steaks on the table. Dakota was one of the first ones to make it up the hill to the table. Margie and Lynn were already seated.

Grace leaned close to him and whispered, "When you get a moment, I need to talk to you." Then she said in a louder voice as the other men approached the table, "Just need to run inside and grab some things." She hurried back toward the deck.

Dakota waited for a moment before following her inside. The house was quiet. Everyone must have been at or headed toward the dinner table. Dakota found Grace in the kitchen. She pulled a piece of paper from her apron. "This was left for me on the kitchen counter." She handed him the note.

Meet me at the shack just past the chairlift at ten p.m. Tuesday. Come alone.
C

"*C* is for *Cory*?" he said.
"Yeah, but why the change of heart?"

"Maybe it's a trap. Maybe someone is putting pressure on him to get me out of the way. Maybe he's not the one who left the note."

Voices in the hallway by the bathroom indicated that at least two people had entered the house.

"Salt and pepper?" The voice was Mrs. Wilson's.

"Yes, sorry, it's on the way." She handed Dakota two sets of salt and pepper shakers and grabbed two more to bring out.

The evening went by quickly. A fire was built in the firepit. Justin and Cory got out guitars. Grace laid out the ingredients for s'mores. Dakota came to stand beside her. The Wilsons let them know they were off duty and free to enjoy the property or turn in for the night.

She let out a heavy breath. "I'm beyond exhausted."

"Me too," he said. "Let's go find out where we sleep."

There was only one private room upstairs, and he guessed that was designated for Mr. and Mrs. Wilson. The other two rooms had bunk beds and twin beds. There were three tents that Dakota had set up outside facing the lake. They chose one of those. The tent had a queen-size air mattress in it that he had inflated earlier.

Grace sighed and fell forward on the bed. "There's no room for you to sleep on the floor." She turned on her side so her back was facing him.

Within minutes, her deep breathing indicated she was asleep. He pulled the covers over her and got into the bed as well. Despite people outside the tent still enjoying the evening, it took him only a few minutes to fall asleep.

He woke up hours later to no more noise from the late-night guests, who must have finally gone to bed. In his sleep, he had rolled closer to Grace. His arm rested across her stomach. The way they used to sleep when they were married.

He lay awake listening in the dark. Someone was moving around outside the tent. Dakota could hear light footsteps and see a hazy shadow. Maybe someone from one of the other tents who needed to use the bathroom in the cabin.

Whoever it was circled the tent and then stood for a long time outside the door before stepping away. Dakota slipped out of the bed and unzipped the door part way. Just in time to see a man headed into the cabin. Someone had been contemplating entering their tent and had thought better of it.

ELEVEN

The remainder of the weekend at the cabin had gone on without incident. Now it was Tuesday night and they were on their way to meet Cory.

Feeling a rising sense of anticipation, Grace checked the clock in her car. She and Dakota had almost an hour to get to the shack by the chairlift. Since the note said that she needed to come alone, they would go in separate cars. Dakota had scouted the location earlier to find a hidden vantage point that would allow him to swoop in if things went south. He hung back in his car. They had made separate excuses to Mr. and Mrs. Wilson as to why they were going out.

It had taken her a while to ferret out what Cory had meant by the shack by the chairlift. Part of the culture of Silver Strike was that people built shacks in the forest that surrounded the ski runs out of odd materials, like old gondolas or cars or scrap materials. Some of the shacks were used as warming sheds but others for more nefarious purposes. Nerves made Grace's mind wander to something positive.

On the second night they were at the cabin, an informal dance had broken out while Cory and Justin played guitar and Evan brought out his set of bongos.

As she drove on the dark road, the memory of Dakota asking her to dance played at the corners of her mind.

He'd whispered in her ear, "We're supposed to look like a happy married couple, remember."

When he held her though, she knew she wasn't entirely pretending. It was easy to feel comfortable in Dakota's arms. Grace shook herself free of the memory and focused on the task ahead.

Seeing the chairlift up ahead, Grace slowed down. She checked her rearview mirror. Dakota had already pulled off into his hiding place. He would approach the remaining distance on foot. Headlights appeared in her rearview mirror. At first, she thought it was Dakota with a change of plans, but the car sped up, coming for her. Heart pounding, she hit the gas. There was no place to turn off—the road led directly to the parking lot. The car rammed her bumper, jarring her.

Turning the wheel tightly, she swung in an arc through the parking lot and then gunned the motor, headed for the surrounding lawn. *Always do the unexpected.*

The car followed her onto the grass. They were both lumbering along on the soft terrain. Her tires spat up grass and dirt when she tried to go faster. She took another turn headed back toward the parking lot in a sort of slow-motion chase.

Dakota had entered the parking lot on foot. He was running toward the other car with his gun raised.

The other car stopped and hit Reverse, backing away over the lawn until it reached an adjoining street and turned around. Dakota continued to run toward it, firing a shot.

Grace drove back into the parking lot. The other car disappeared down a side street. Dakota ran a short ways after it then slowed down and ran back to where she was.

Her heart was still racing from the incident as she rested her head on the back of the seat.

Dakota came over to her car and swung open the passenger's side door and got in, leaning toward her. "You okay?"

She nodded. "Just a little shook-up. What was that about?"

"An ambush to hurt you. Maybe the note from Cory was fake to get us out here."

"It's another half hour before we're supposed to meet Cory. Either we were followed from the house or Cory set that up. That guy came out on a side road. He must have figured out where I was going and took a shortcut to ambush me."

"Do you think Cory is still going to show?"

"I think we should keep the appointment." She was still waiting for her heart rate to return to normal. "You know how the drug trade works. Turf wars and all that. We could be dealing with more than one player."

He pushed open the door and stepped out then came around the vehicle to open the door for her. When she got out, her knees buckled. He grasped her elbows.

"Whoa, guess I'm a little more shook-up than I realized." As she stood facing him, she realized her concentration had been off because she'd been thinking about dancing with Dakota. That's why the attack had taken her by surprise. She took a step back. In a job like this, losing focus could be deadly. Whatever growing feelings she had for Dakota, she needed to set them aside.

Though she could admit that being around Dakota, being held by him, felt like the most natural thing in the world. She knew that if they were to get back together, there would always be that underlying fear that when she needed him most he would leave. Though it was not his doing, every time she looked at him, she thought of Anita.

"Let's head up to the rendezvous point then," said Dakota. He touched his chest where his shoulder holster was. "Remember, I've got your back."

They separated. She moved up the hill out in the open, and he worked his way through trees and brush. If they were being watched from a high vantage point, whoever was watching would know that she was not alone, just like whoever had been in that car knew Dakota was in this with her. It was a twenty-minute hike up the hill.

She was out of breath by the time she arrived at the shack, which looked like it was constructed from scrap pieces of wood and metal. She used the flashlight on her phone to illuminate the interior of the shack. The walls were decorated with old skis and there was a bench also made out of skis. No Cory. There was only one way in and out of the shack. To go inside and wait would make her too vulnerable a target. She sat down near the open doorway and waited, listening to the night sounds around her. She texted Dakota her status.

She checked her watch. It was five minutes past the time Cory should have arrived. The shack didn't provide a view of the parking lot below, and the surrounding trees meant someone moving stealthily could get very close to her before she would be aware of their presence.

She was grateful that Dakota was close by.

A buzzing noise in the interior of the shack caused her to whirl around and peek inside. A light flashed. There was something on the bench. She aimed her flashlight. A phone. She hadn't noticed it in the dim cabin at first. The buzz had sounded like a text message being received. She detected a vibrating sound. Someone calling.

She hesitated in stepping into the shack. First, because it made her vulnerable to attack, and second, because she feared the phone was a bomb.

The phone stopped vibrating.

She stepped back and looked around. Dakota could see her even if she couldn't see him. She made a hand signal indicating that he needed to come to her. He was so quiet in approaching her she didn't see him until he was only a few feet away.

"What is going on?"

"I don't think Cory is going to show, but there is a phone in the shack. Someone texted and called so I would notice it."

"I'll go inside. You stand watch." He slipped past her.

Dakota knew the risk he was taking. She stepped a little farther away from the shack. Her chest squeezed tight. If it was a bomb, he could die. He was willing to do that so she would be safe.

He stepped out still holding the phone. "You want to stay back. I'm going to see who tried to contact you."

He clicked a button on the phone. She squeezed her eyes shut, bracing for an explosion. She took in a sharp breath. "No, wait." She didn't want to live in a world without Dakota.

"Grace, whatever happens, it will be okay. You'll be okay."

"I don't want you to die. At least pray first, Dakota. And so will I."

"Okay. God, we pray for safety and that Your will be done. Amen."

"Amen."

Dakota clicked the buttons on the phone. He stared down at the screen. "It's a text message from whoever Cory was a courier for. It says 'Congratulations, Grace. To get out, Cory supplied you as his replacement. Keep this phone with you. I will give you your first assignment shortly. Once the assignment is complete, throw the phone away.'"

Dakota looked up at her. "Looks like you're in." He leaned a little closer to her. "You okay?"

For three years since she'd been taking these assignments, she'd always felt a sense of victory once she was able to infiltrate some part of a drug-trafficking network. "Guess I'm just feeling a little afraid." The fear was new. It had to be connected to her caring whether she lived or died. "You know, after I see this investigation to the end, I don't think I'm going to sign up for the dangerous assignments anymore."

He studied her for a long moment. He reached up and touched her face, trailing his finger down her cheek. "Welcome back to life, Gracie Girl. I had to make the same journey."

She gazed into his eyes as a sense of warmth flooded through her. "I'm glad you are here with me, Dakota."

He took his hand away from her face and stepped

back, breaking the moment of connection. He handed her the phone. "Do you think this is legit?"

"What do you mean?"

"Any time you talked directly to Cory, he didn't want to let you in on a piece of the pie. The note, the phone call—how do we know he had anything to do with them?"

"I don't know. That's the nature of undercover work, not having all the answers. I just know we got to play along if we are to figure out who is behind all this."

Dakota nodded. "You know my impression of Cory is that he didn't want you involved because he wouldn't wish his life on anyone. Like he wanted to protect you from your life becoming like his."

"I agree. Being around him all weekend, I didn't think he was a bad guy, just messed up."

"We better get back to the Wilson house before we're missed," he said.

They walked through the trees and headed down the hill to the parking lot. Still aware that they might be watched, Dakota moved down separately from her, staying closer to the trees out of view.

She arrived at her car, unlocked the doors and reached for the door handle. Just as she squeezed the handle and pulled on it, she noticed the flashing light inside the car. She saw the wire that connected to the door. A crude bomb. The understanding sparked inside her brain in less than a second. She knew too the bomb had been activated by her opening the door.

Intense force and heat surrounded her as the explosion blew her backward. She was lifted up and thrown down, landing on her bottom. The car door sailed through the air toward her. She rolled to get out of the way. The door clattered against the asphalt inches from her. Even as she rose to her feet, shock spread through her.

Dakota was beside her, dragging her away from the wreckage. "Leave it here. Come with me to my car."

She shook her head. Though the rest of the car was intact, the entire driver's seat was blown apart. If she had not seen the blinking light… The bomber had intended to kill her.

The car had been the one they'd driven from Seattle. Dakota had come in one of Mr. Wilson's cars. Dakota pulled out his phone. "We'll get DEA out here to take it in for evidence. We need to get back. We'll just tell the Wilsons your car broke down and is in a shop. In a couple of days, we'll say the car couldn't be fixed."

"This doesn't make any sense. I've just agreed to be a courier. Why try to kill me, unless we are dealing with more than one player?"

"I'm not sure what's going on either. But like you said, we've got to play this through until the end."

They walked the remaining distance to where Dakota had hidden his car.

Grace was still trying to process everything that had happened. She reached to open the passenger's side door.

"Wait. Let me have a look around the car first," said Dakota. He stuck his head underneath the car and used the flashlight on his phone.

She walked around the car checking the interior for any signs of another bomb, looking for wires, a box, anything that looked out of place.

"We can't be too careful, Grace." Dakota cautiously

opened the driver's side door and shone his light underneath the dashboard.

Satisfied, both of them got in the car. Dakota turned the key in the ignition without incident. He drove through the streets of Silver Strike, which were mostly dark, except for some bars and restaurants. Once they arrived at the Wilson house, he clicked on the garage door opener while the car idled and then drove inside the garage, which stored five cars and a motorcycle that belonged to Justin.

Grace had placed the phone that would link her to the drug network in her coat pocket. As they walked back in the house, the weight of it pressed against her stomach. If whoever orchestrated the trafficking only communicated via text, she wasn't sure how to move the investigation forward. They needed face-to-face contact. That meant months of building trust.

Tomorrow she would get in touch with DEA with the number the call and text had come from. But she had the feeling it would be from a throwaway phone.

Dakota punched in the alarm code that would get them into the house. They stepped into a hallway that led to the kitchen.

Mrs. Wilson stood in the kitchen. A dish of the leftover enchiladas Grace had cooked for dinner sat on the counter. Cindy Wilson held a phone in hand and spoke into it. "Gotta go, bye." She looked up when they entered the open area of the living room and kitchen.

"You caught me having a late-night snack," she said. Her long blond hair was pulled up in a careless ponytail.

Mrs. Wilson seemed guilty or secretive.

"You're up late," said Dakota, keeping his tone friendly. "I couldn't stop thinking about Grace's enchiladas."

Mrs. Wilson glanced first at Grace and then Dakota. "You two came home together? I thought you went in separate cars because you were going different places."

"Grace's car broke down. She called me to come get her. It's going to be in the shop for a while."

Mrs. Wilson nodded. "You two have a good night." Her tone was dismissive, indicating she didn't want to talk anymore.

Once they were in their bedroom and changed into pajamas, Grace set the phone on the nightstand by the couch. It was her turn to sleep there. "Mrs. Wilson was acting kind of funny."

"Yeah, right before dinner I overheard her and Mr. Wilson having a heated discussion about the credit card bill and her spending. It's the only hint I've picked up on any financial struggle. And it might just be that Mr. Wilson thinks her spending is out of control."

She fluffed her pillow. "They don't seem very happy when they're together."

Dakota shrugged. "He works a lot. Even when he's home, he's on that laptop or a phone."

Her throat constricted. His words felt like a stab to her heart. "I know what that's like. A man who buries himself in his work." She braced herself for an angry or defensive response, which was what she had always gotten when they were married.

Dakota's shoulders slumped. He came and sat beside her on the couch. "I'm so sorry that I did that to you. We both were not coping very well and we should have been there for each other."

Grace felt all her defenses slip away. Her remark had been so filled with pain that it came across as cutting and yet his words were so gentle. She reached over and covered his hand with hers. "You've really changed, Dakota…in a really beautiful way."

"It's not me…really. After everything fell apart, I was so broken and lost. God just got a hold of my heart."

"I feel like that is happening for me too."

He turned to face her. "I know it can."

The warmth in his eyes drew her in.

"Would it make you feel better if I held you?"

She nodded. He wrapped his arms around her. She nuzzled against his chest, relishing the musky smell of his skin. He stroked her hair. Tears rimmed her eyes and rolled down her cheeks. She wasn't even sure why she was crying. But it felt like some of the grief and pain she'd pushed down for so long was leaving her body with each tear.

After a while, Dakota released her from the embrace. He drew her close and kissed her forehead, got up from the couch, and pulled the covers back on the bed. She lay down on the bed, pulling the covers around her. She fell asleep thinking that was the kindest thing anyone had ever done for her.

At six a.m. the phone for the drug contact buzzed. While she was waking up and grappling for the phone, Dakota's phone dinged that he had a text as well.

Dakota reached for his phone. Was it possible it was a coincidence they were both getting messages at the same time?

was on the south side. They'd have to walk through the crowded market to get to the pottery booth.

Once they were through the parking lot, they split up, walking through parallel aisles of the market. The market was crowded. A noisy band blasted music from a nearby pavilion while people gathered on the grass to eat and listen. The booths sold mostly crafts with a few produce booths that must have come from greenhouses. It was too early for any outdoor crops. The food vendors were intermixed with the other booths. People mingled, hugged and clumped together in conversation. The aroma of both salty and sweet foods cooking floated in the air.

Grace had worn a distinct-looking yellow dress so she'd be easy to spot in the crowd. Twice though Dakota lost sight of her as she worked her way toward the other end of the market. The first time, she'd merely slipped around the other side of a booth because she'd seen something that interested her.

The second time, his heart squeezed tight when he watched a cluster of people surround her. When the crowd dispersed, he'd lost sight of her. He scanned the sea of faces, watching the casual interaction of people while he grew more tense.

Trying to appear unalarmed, he ambled toward the aisle where he'd last seen her. He feigned interest in a booth that sold items made of leather. He scanned the entire area trying to spot the yellow of the dress. He walked a little faster then stopped suddenly when he saw her.

She was kneeling, helping a woman pick up a bunch of flowers that had fallen out of a vase that lay broken on the ground.

Dakota strode past her. He bought a hot dog, watching her in his peripheral vision.

Confident she wasn't going anywhere for a minute while she helped the woman pick up the pieces of the broken vase, he took a glance around at the people. Across two rows of booths he spotted Justin Wilson and his friend Evan. Justin was turned sideways, and Evan had his back to Dakota. Dakota slipped behind the hot dog booth. The two men meandered away from the booths toward the pavilion where the concert was taking place.

Interesting. Silver Strike was not that big a town. It made sense that an event like a farmers market would attract anyone who was looking for something to do. Still, the timing of them being here was a bit suspect. Also, Cory was not with them. He hadn't seen Cory since the weekend at the cabin.

Grace put the flowers in a new vase and set them with the other flowers the woman had for sale before she continued through the market.

He kept eyes on her from two booths away. She arrived at the Big Sky Bowls and Stuff booth. The woman manning the booth was maybe in her forties. She wore a scarf on her head.

Dakota positioned himself so he could take pictures of the woman and appear like he was just shooting the color and activity of the market and had accidently gotten her in the shot.

Grace must have been aware of where he was because she stepped to one side so he had a clear view of the vendor. The woman might be an innocent in all this, but they still needed to check her out.

Grace leaned in and spoke to the woman, who turned and bent over to grab something by a table leg.

Dakota tensed. Given the attempts on their lives already, he had to assume everything was a trap. Shooting Grace in the crowded market was unlikely but spraying her with a slow-acting poison or touching her skin with it was not.

The woman handed Grace a colorful bag. Grace unzipped it and peeked inside. Satisfied, she zipped it back up. She spoke to the woman a moment longer and then pivoted to work her way back through the market.

They met at the car. "Why the zippered pouch?" He opened the driver's side door.

"The woman put it in there. She was afraid the envelope would get torn or lost."

"What was your impression of the woman?"

"She said a man came by just as the market was opening and offered her twenty dollars if she would hold the envelope until I showed up." Grace got into the car as well. "I did ask her if she could describe that man."

"And?" He turned the key in the ignition.

"She said he was older and wore a straw hat."

That didn't sound like Justin or Evan. They could have been in disguise or gotten someone else to drop the envelope off. "That's all?"

"She said he was completely unmemorable. Nothing distinct about him."

The description could just as well have been Mr. Wilson. "I saw Justin and Evan but no Cory."

"He hasn't been around since that weekend at the cabin." Grace stared down at the zippered bag and then touched her hand to her heart.

"I know this is scary, but we're in this together." He

pulled out of the parking lot and merged with traffic on the two-lane road that led back to the Wilson house.

She let out a heavy breath. "The fear is new for me, remember. I was just thinking that maybe this will be my last dangerous assignment. I'll go back to intel gathering."

He smiled at her. "I'm glad to hear that. I'm looking forward to getting back to the Coast Guard."

After driving for about five minutes, the Wilson house came into view. He clicked the automatic garage door opener and drove in. The realization hit him that there would be a time when he and Grace would be parting ways if they got out of this alive.

For most of the afternoon, Grace's stomach remained tied up in knots. She pulled the envelope from the zippered pouch and put it in her purse along with the contact phone. She and Dakota had a quiet afternoon while they waited for the hour when they would drive with Mr. Wilson to the airport.

Dakota had gone with Mr. Wilson to play a couple rounds of golf to blow off some steam before the flight. She knew Dakota would use the opportunity to gather information.

Though she didn't need to do any meal prep, she kept busy in the kitchen putting together snacks for the people on the plane. As far as she knew, there was no one else in the house. As she headed back down the hall to the room she and Dakota shared, her footsteps seemed to echo.

A door slammed somewhere upstairs. Her heart beat a little faster. She grabbed her gun from the room and headed back down the hall and up the stairs. She searched the rooms that had open doors.

The second floor had a veranda that looked out on the golf course. A man sat in one of the lounge chairs. She could see only the top of his head. She shoved the gun in her waistband, covering it with her shirt hem.

She eased the door to the veranda open and stepped toward the lounge chairs.

"I didn't realize anyone else was here."

The man jerked around, planting his bare feet on the floor. It was Justin. He stared at her long enough that it made her feel uncomfortable. "I didn't want to deal with my father, so I slipped in the back way and snuck up to my room to get some shut-eye." He pointed out toward the golf course. "But I see he's out enjoying himself with your husband."

Justin was a thirty-year-old man, yet his behavior toward his father was like that of a teenager.

"You and your father are fighting?"

Justin put his feet back up on the lounge chair. "It's the usual stuff about how I'm not doing anything with my life. It's not just the cruise line that he owns. He's got his fingers in these other businesses and he wants me to take over some of it, but not until I—" he mimed air quotes *"—show signs of being a grown-up."*

Sensing an opportunity, she sat down in the lounge chair next to Justin's. "And you don't want to do that?"

Again, his gaze rested on her long enough to make her feel uncomfortable. "He just has a different defini-tion of *grown-up.*"

She nodded, trying to let him think she understood and was on his side. "I haven't seen Cory around in a few days. You guys were joined at the hip when Dakota and I first came here."

Justin shrugged. "Cory was messed up. I think he went somewhere to get straightened out."

She didn't want to press. Asking too many questions might raise alarm bells if Justin was in any way connected with the trafficking.

She rose to her feet. "I suppose I better go finish packing. Sorry to hear you're not going on the trip since you are his son."

"Like I said. Hanging out with my father while he works isn't my idea of a good time." His anger was almost visceral.

"Well, I'll see you when we get back." If they came back. She had a feeling that returning to Seattle would move them toward a conclusion to all of this. She walked the short distance to the door that connected with the second floor. When she glanced backward, Justin was watching her in a way that made the hairs on the back of her neck prickle.

THIRTEEN

To cut out the setting sun, Dakota put his sunglasses on and then helped load the baggage of the other passengers. Mr. Wilson, his daughter Lynn, and granddaughter, Margie, had all boarded the plane along with the pilot.

Grace handed him the last suitcase. She kept the purse that contained the package close to her. She winked at him as if to offer him reassurance that everything was okay. She must have picked up on his trepidation.

The gesture warmed his heart. The saddest thing about their marriage falling apart was that even at the time, he knew that Grace was truly a decent human being. The grief, the tragedy of unbearable loss had just made everything impossible. They had been like two people stumbling around trying to find each other in the dark.

They boarded the plane as the propellers started to whir. They were seated in the back two seats behind Lynn and Margie. He wanted to tell Grace that while he was playing golf with Mr. Wilson, Wilson had let slip about some financial struggles and that this meeting in Seattle was to try to get things straightened out, but he hadn't had the chance.

Margie whirled around and smiled at them, a gesture that would have made anyone smile back.

But it just caused a pain in the pit of his stomach. He knew that being around the sweet little girl had the same effect on Grace. Grace's smile was more like a spasm than a smile.

"Margie, sit down," Lynn said.

Dakota reached for Grace's hand and squeezed it. She looked at him with wide blue eyes. Her lips were drawn into a hard straight line, indicating the level of pain she felt by being around Margie. He held on to her hand.

The plane taxied forward on the runway and stopped until they were cleared for take-off. The plane rolled forward, gaining speed. All of them were silent until the plane lifted and leveled off. It was a small enough plane that each gust of wind made it wobble in the sky.

Margie started to fuss, wiggling in her seat.

Grace cleared her throat. "I put together some fun snacks for Margie. I know how restless kids can get at that age on long car and plane rides. I have some rice cakes and other things so she can make happy faces and then eat them."

Dakota raised his eyebrows and gave her hand a squeeze. Grace was trying to work through the pain that being around Margie caused. He had to admire her.

Lynn let out a heavy sigh. "That would be great. You can sit in my seat. I'll go up and talk to Dad."

Grace retrieved the snacks she'd prepared and sat beside Margie, folding both tray tables down.

Dakota listened while Grace set out a rice cake, a container of cream cheese and various veggies to make the happy face. Margie laughed as she decided to use olive slices for eyes and a piece of red pepper for the smile. As he listened to the interaction between the little girl and the woman who used to be his wife, his eyes rimmed with tears. Memories of Anita flooded through his mind.

Dakota unbuckled his seat belt and retreated to the bathroom. He splashed water on his face. Grace was being brave; she was trying to push through her pain. After Anita's death, he'd taken every dangerous assignment, been away for weeks at a time and never shed a tear. Maybe one of the reasons he'd run away was because Grace couldn't stop crying. As he stood alone in the bathroom, he let the tears flow. Though he remained silent, he cried out to God. He released the pain over losing their little girl that had been bottled up for three years. When he returned to his seat, Grace was holding Margie while she slept. Instead of sitting behind them, he took the seat opposite them. Grace smiled up at him while she held the sleeping toddler.

There would always be a hole in both of them for the loss but maybe they could come together in that pain instead of tear each other apart like they had done before.

The flight took less than two hours. The sky was dusty gray when they touched down. Once the plane had landed, Dakota retrieved the rental car and helped load baggage. Mr. Wilson sat in the front with Dakota while the two women and Margie sat in the back.

They were driving through the city toward the hotel where Mr. Wilson had reservations when Grace's phone beeped. She took it out of her purse and read the text.

Dakota glanced in the rearview mirror just as Grace

looked up from her phone. Her face had drained of color and he saw fear in her eyes.

Grace clicked off the phone and put it away as her stomach twisted into knots. She had been given instructions to leave the package in a car in a parking garage at midnight.

Though she kept her eyes open and watched the city at night flash by, she found herself praying that everything would go smoothly. That the drop-off would open more doors to discover who was behind all this.

Margie, who was sitting in between her and Lynn, kicked her feet in her car seat and then tugged on Grace's sleeve, offering Grace a big smile before turning her head playfully away.

"She's really taken with you," said Lynn.

"I'm quite taken with her." Grace pressed her face close to Margie's. "'Cause she's a sweetie."

For the first time since Anita's death, Grace felt as though her heart had been freed from a confining cage. Grief was not something you got over; it was something you walked through.

Lynn smiled and gazed out the window, and Grace's mind shifted to what she had to do tonight. A thousand things could go wrong with a drop-off. It was clear that someone in Montana had wanted to wipe her and Dakota out of the equation. It was possible that person had followed them here or had contacted someone who could finish the job.

Dakota hit his blinker and headed toward the hotel. Mr. Wilson had talked on his phone to business associates for the entire drive. After the luggage was unloaded, the valet took the car. Grace stepped in beside

Dakota. She would not be able to tell him the specifics of the text until they were alone. Once they were upstairs, she was grateful to see that she and Dakota had been given a separate but adjoining suite.

The main suite had a kitchenette that connected with two sleeping areas. Grace laid out the remainder of the snacks she'd prepared ahead of time.

"Are you going to want me to put together anything else?" she asked Lynn since Mr. Wilson was still on his phone.

"I think we'll be okay for tonight," said Lynn. "Daddy always wants to take care of everything for us but tends to choose poorly when it comes to room service and restaurants, so if you could put together a breakfast for tomorrow. I think he's doing lunch and dinner with clients. At least one of those meals will be in the suite."

"I'll do the shopping tonight. Is it okay if Dakota drives me?"

She looked over at Mr. Wilson, who nodded, pulling the phone away from his face. "I'm in for the rest of the evening."

Getting groceries would be the perfect cover for making the drop-off. After saying good-night to the family, she went to her room. Dakota was waiting for her, sitting in a chair that looked out on water. The hotel was close to a harbor. He had his phone in his hand.

She felt a sense of relief now that they were alone. She opened up her phone and read him the address. It was a little before ten o'clock. "There will be a white compact car in space number thirty-four. The doors will be unlocked. I'm to put the package in the back seat and walk away. The usual instructions to come alone, not tell anyone and be unarmed."

"But you won't be alone." He winked at her then looked at his phone. "The parking garage is about ten minutes from here. If you want to take a nap, I'll wake you up."

Not sure if she'd be able to sleep, she lay down on top of the covers and closed her eyes. Despite the fear of what they faced, she felt herself drifting off.

What felt like ten minutes later, Dakota was squeezing her shoulder. "Time to go, Gracie."

Dakota had not yet put his jacket on. The gun in the shoulder holster reminded her of the level of danger they faced. As per the instructions, she would not have a gun but she knew Dakota would have her back.

They took the elevator to the lobby and waited while the valet brought the rental car around. She rested the purse with the package on her legs. "I'm supposed to ditch the phone as soon as I make the drop-off."

"Throw it in a trash can where DEA can pick it up. These guys are careful. I doubt that Forensics will find anything, but we can't leave loose ends."

She reached over and patted his leg. "I'm glad that you're here with me."

"Me too," he said. "Be careful tonight."

"I'll do my best." Hopefully, this was as simple as the text made it sound. Drug dealers were notorious for their paranoia and their lack of loyalty. If a rival dealer or someone looking to take over had knowledge of the drop-off, things could go sideways.

Dakota drove to the parking garage and up to the third level. He circled around.

"There it is. There's the white car," she said.

Dakota's voice was very solemn. "I'll circle around and park on the other side. I'll be right behind you but out of view."

She nodded. They parked and got out. Grace walked out in the open but on high alert. Her footsteps seemed to echo on the concrete. When she peered over her shoulder, she saw Dakota slip between two parked cars.

The open-air garage looked out on the harbor. She could smell the salt air as it wafted in from the sea.

She came around a curve. The white car was within view.

A man with a gun stepped out from the side of the car next to the white car. "I think you should hand me that." He had blond slicked-back hair. Grace didn't recognize him.

Grace took a step back, clutching the purse. "I don't know who you are, but that's not the plan."

"Give me the package." The man lifted the gun so it was aimed right at her chest.

She knew Dakota was close by and would step in if needed. The first option was always to try to talk her way out of this and to get as much information as possible about why this man knew about the drop-off.

"Look, I'm just a courier. If I don't follow orders, I don't get paid." It seemed odd to her that the man hadn't just waited until she dropped off the envelope to take it. "How did you know I'd be here?"

"I got my orders too." He stepped toward her with his hand out, still aiming the gun at her. "Now hand it over."

Maybe the man had only enough information to know that she'd be here, not that she was going to leave the envelope in the unlocked car.

Her heart raced as a rising sense of panic filled her.

Or maybe the intent all along had been to get her into a vulnerable place and shoot her.

Dakota peered out from the side of the car where the shadows hid him. His legs were tensed, ready to spring up and run into a position where he could get a clean shot at the guy. He knew he had to allow time for Grace to talk the man out of shooting her and gain some information by keeping him engaged in conversation. Grace could handle herself. She'd been in these kinds of situations before. But he could hardly bear seeing that gun pointed at her. The need to protect her was so intense.

Grace was good at reading people; she knew when they would attack and when they were bluffing, and she had the training to defend herself. He had to give her a moment.

She opened the purse and pulled out the envelope. "Who are you working for? Maybe we're on the same side here."

The man's posture stiffened as he tightened his grip on the gun. His body language said he was through talking.

Dakota jumped to his feet and sprinted toward the man with the gun, raising his gun to shoot. The guy whirled around, aiming his gun at Dakota. Grace lunged at him, hitting him in the back. His hand jerked up and the shot went into the ceiling. The man grabbed for the envelope. She held on. It tore. The contents spilled across the concrete. Not money. Not drugs. Pieces of cut-up newspaper.

Shock spread through her.

This whole thing was a setup. What was going on here?

The taillights of the white car flared to life. Someone

was behind the wheel. The car backed toward Grace. She jumped out of the way.

The man with the gun aimed at them again.

Dakota pushed her toward the shelter of the parked cars as another shot pinged off the concrete pillars. The man with the gun came directly at them. As they wove between the cars and ran toward the next row, Dakota could hear the white car circling around, tires squealing, seeking to cut them off.

His heart pounded as he held on tight to Grace's hand. They wouldn't be able to make it back to their car without getting caught or shot.

Grace tugged on his hand. "The elevator."

They ran through the two rows of cars parked facing each other. Dakota could see the shooter's blond head bobbing up three car lengths behind them. They couldn't get to the elevator without being shot.

They were beside a van that was high off the ground. He slipped underneath the van. Grace rolled in beside him. He could hear the white car circling and the footsteps of the man with the gun as he searched for them. He stomped past. He must not have seen them drop down under the van.

Dakota rolled out from underneath the van; crouching low by the next car hid him from view. Grace pressed in beside him. He listened, trying to detect where the shooter was. His footsteps grew more faint. He was backtracking, trying to figure out where they'd gone.

Now was their chance. There was only one more car between them and the elevator. He worked his way down the length of the car and then along the bumper.

He burst to his feet and took off running. Grace's footsteps pounded behind him.

He was within ten feet of the elevator when car tires squealed off to the side of him. He sprinted and slammed against the wall where the elevator buttons were. He pressed the down button. He could hear the cables in the elevator working as it traveled down to the third floor.

Grace's panicked voice reached him. "He's behind us."

He dove to the ground, as did Grace. The elevator door slid open slowly. He craned his neck. The man with the gun was stalking toward them, getting close enough to have an accurate shot with a pistol. When the door was open only a foot and a half they crawled into the elevator. Dakota flipped around and fired a shot.

The man shot back. Both of them retreated behind the still-open door for cover on opposite sides of the elevator. He caught a glimpse of the man raising his gun just as the doors closed.

Grace let out a heavy breath and stared at the ceiling. "We were set up."

The number two lit up above the elevator panel.

"I know," he said. "Maybe they've wanted us dead all along. If that's the case, the question we need to be asking is *why?* I just can't believe that anyone would have figured out we were DEA. How could they? The only other option is we are dealing with someone who is very territorial and sees us as a threat."

The elevator came to a stop on the first floor of the parking garage. The doors slid open. Both of them rose to their feet, resting a supportive hand on the padded wall. They stepped out, glancing around nervously.

The gunman could have taken the stairs and got to the ground floor first.

"What do you think? We wait it out and go back up and get the car." Her voice wavered.

They walked through the silent parking garage. "Let's get an Uber. Go get the groceries you need for tomorrow. We have a part to play, remember."

"I know, but part of not looking suspicious is coming back in that rental car."

"I don't think it's safe to go back to that car," he said. "Maybe I'll just have to rent a car of the same model."

They stepped out onto the street. There were not many streetlamps in this part of town. Dakota pulled his phone out, squinting to see.

Grace grabbed his shoulder and squeezed. "We got a problem."

The white car emerged from the parking garage, gaining speed and headed in their direction.

FOURTEEN

The car barreled toward them onto the sidewalk, head-lights nearly blinding Grace. Sprinting with all their strength, she and Dakota veered away from the side-walk across the grass toward the harbor. The car fol-lowed them partway but then took a sharp turn. She doubted the driver was giving up.

The ground they ran across was saturated from the rain that must have happened earlier in the day. The driver probably realized he'd get stuck and was going to get to the harbor some safer way. Any thought of backtracking was destroyed when the car slowed to a crawl. The man with the gun got out of the back seat and ran toward them.

The harbor was filled with shipping containers. Large boats resting on the water along with some smaller ones that may have been fishing vessels bobbed up and down. They ran through the maze of shipping containers and hid in between two that were close together.

Grace pressed her back against the cold metal of the shipping container. They were squeezed in so tightly that she could not fully extend her arm. The man with the gun ran past them.

Shuffling sideways, they worked their way out to the other side of the container, which was close to the water. At this hour, the yard was shut down. She saw one man walking the deck of a ship some distance from them.

She peeked out from around the shipping container. She spotted the man with the gun right away, though the gun was no longer visible. He probably didn't want to raise alarm bells if he was spotted. Though she did not see security guards anywhere, places like this usually had at least one.

Dakota pressed against her. "That must be the guy that was in the white car," he whispered in her ear and pointed.

The other man must not have been able to bring his car down to the harbor or it must've been easier to look for them on foot. It was clear he was searching for them. He was stalking around in a different area of the yard. He stopped, staring in their direction. Both of them slipped back behind the cargo container.

Grace's heart rate kicked up a notch. "Do you think he saw us?"

"We can't take the chance." Dakota was already scooting toward the other end of the container.

She followed, glancing over her shoulder. Her stomach clenched. The man was coming toward the container. They'd been spotted.

Dakota sprinted toward the water's edge. He made a splashing sound as he dove in between boats. She jumped in behind him. The chill of the water enveloped and shocked her. They were between two ships that towered two or three stories above them. Dakota's head bobbed to the surface as he swam out to the stern of the boat. She dove underwater and followed him, not sure exactly what his plan was.

When she came up for air, she caught a glimpse of the man on shore walking past. She swam to the end of the boat. Dakota trod water, pressing close to the hull of the boat.

"Let's swim around a couple more boats and see if it's safe to get to shore."

She could feel a chill settling in to her bones. "Okay, but I don't think we should stay in the water much longer."

He nodded and dove under. As she swam beneath the surface of the water, her muscles started to cramp from the cold. She came up for air. She couldn't see Dakota anywhere, but she heard a splash closer to the shore. She swam toward where the noise had come from.

The water remained deep as she got closer to the shore where there was a four-foot concrete wall. She had to assume that Dakota had already pulled himself out of the water. Her teeth were chattering as she reached up for the top of the concrete wall. Dakota was there. He pulled her up. They had swum almost to the other end of the harbor. There were only a couple of small boats at this end. Up the hill, she could see the faint lights of the parking garage.

Dakota wrapped his arms around her. "I know you're cold."

She glanced down toward the shipping containers. Though it was fairly dark, she didn't see anyone moving around searching for them.

"Where do you two think you're going?" They whirled around as a bright light shone in their faces.

"Shipyard security. You two better come with me. The Feds are looking for you."

The security guard aimed his gun at Dakota. "Open your coat. Are you armed?"

Dakota obliged.

"Toss your weapon over on the ground there."

Not seeing any way out of the situation that didn't involve one of them being shot, Dakota complied.

Dakota's thoughts raced a hundred miles an hour as the security guard escorted them to a small room without windows.

"You two look like you could use some dry clothes. Give me a minute," said the security guard.

The guard, an overweight man probably in his forties, clicked the lock into place.

"What does he mean the Feds are looking for us?" Grace, who was still shivering, crossed her arms over her chest and paced in the small room.

"I have my suspicions," said Dakota. There were two benches in the room and a table with a coffee maker on it. This must have been the break/detention room.

"You think those guys after us said they were federal agents?"

Dakota nodded. "It couldn't be the real Feds unless DEA communicated with them. How would they even know we were here?" He continued to look around the small room. There were two doors, one a supply closet, the other a small bathroom.

She slumped down on the bench. "I suppose it would be nothing for them to flash a badge in front of the security guard. I doubt he has much training or looked closely."

The door clicked open and the security guard tossed in some clothes. His hand was on the gun in his side holster. "You have five minutes to get changed," he added then shut the door.

Grace picked up a shirt and pair of sweats. "I have to get out of these wet clothes. You should too. Aren't you cold?"

"Yes, but I need a minute to figure out a plan of attack."

She retreated to the bathroom. He slipped out of his wet shirt and picked up the dry one. He checked the supply closet again. There wasn't anything they could throw at the guard to distract him when he opened the door. He spoke to Grace through the closed door while he peeled off his soaked pants and put on the dry ones. "We have to try to take that guard when he opens the door. It's our only chance." And hope the two men weren't right behind him with their guns.

"Okay." Grace stepped out of the bathroom. Both the shirt and sweats looked baggy on her.

They both startled when they heard the dead bolt turning. They took up positions by either side of the door. Grace stood by where the door would swing open. She would have a view of the connecting room. What Dakota was counting on was that the security guard had minimal training and that they would be led to the "agents" in a different room.

The door swung open. The security guard had his weapon drawn as he stepped back. "Come out one at a time, hands up where I can see them."

Dakota glanced at Grace. She shook her head. Dakota's hope deflated like a balloon losing air. She stepped across the threshold with her hands in the air. He followed behind her, assuming the same posture.

The two men masquerading as agents stood in the corner of the larger room looking very smug. Both men had shoulder holsters that were visible.

"Thank you, officer," said the man who had been hiding in the white car. He had a scar above his left eyebrow.

The security guard lifted his chin, looking very satisfied. "All in a night's work, gentlemen."

"You two, come with us," said the other man, who had blond slicked-back hair.

The fake agents thanked the security guard again.

Dakota hoped maybe alarm bells would go off for the security guard. "It's standard procedure to handcuff a suspect."

Grace looked toward the security guard. "Please. These men are not who they say they are."

The security guard blinked as though he were trying to process what they were saying. His forehead furrowed as he looked at Dakota and then at the man with the scar above his eye.

Blondie stepped in. "We have twisty ties that we use to restrain them." He looked over at the man with the scar. "Isn't that right, Randy?"

Randy took the ties out of his pocket. "Hauling cuffs around would have drawn attention to our undercover work."

Randy pulled his gun. "These guys have been wanted for a long time."

Satisfied, the security guard nodded while both Grace and Dakota had their hands restrained behind their backs.

They were led to the white car and placed in the back seat.

Randy tapped Dakota on the forehead. "Don't try anything."

The two men got into the front seat and headed toward the street.

Grace gave Dakota a pensive look. She tilted her head toward the seat belt. Neither of them had been buckled in. Even if they could get turned sideways, open the door and roll out, they would be caught or shot before they got to their feet and ran away.

"We got to get rid of these guys," said Blondie.

"Water is always the best bet. Bodies won't be found," said Randy.

Dakota struggled to focus on getting out of the situation. How much time did they have before the men found a secluded place to shoot them and toss their bodies into the harbor?

"Remember we got to get a picture or we don't get paid," said Blondie.

Both men laughed, a sound that sent chills down his spine. So they were hired muscle. By whom? he wondered.

Dakota saw fear in Grace's eyes. He wanted to tell her not to give up hope, but any conversation could bring wrath down on them. He simply lifted his chin, praying his eyes communicated that he would find a way to get them out of this.

They drove through the streets, leaving an industrial part of town to an area with flashing neon, places that were open all night. The streets were crowded with people. Nothing in what he saw suggested the neighborhood was a safe one.

The light in front of them turned red and Randy hit the brakes. He tapped the steering wheel nervously. A man plastered his face against the windshield then drew out a squeegee and started to wash the windshield.

Randy rolled down the window. "Get off there."

The man persisted in his cleaning activity. Another man came up to the window and shoved his hand through it. The distraction was an answer to his prayer.

Grace, who was seated closest to the sidewalk, had already shifted so she could open the door. She tumbled out and wobbled to her feet then headed toward the sidewalk. It took Dakota a moment longer.

The light turned green.

Grace hurried along the sidewalk and stepped through the first open door she came to. Dakota was right behind her. The last thing he saw before stepping into the dark room was Blondie getting out of the car while Randy sped forward, probably to find a parking space so he could help in hunting them down.

The building they had entered was dark and smelled musty. Dakota heard someone coughing in the darkness. He could just make out some makeshift beds and old mattresses. This must be a building where homeless people squatted.

Knowing he had only seconds before Blondie came looking for them, Dakota slipped behind a pile of boxes. Grace must have found a hiding place as well.

He heard footsteps. A light flashed.

Someone yelled, "Hey, get out of here with those bright lights. People are trying to sleep."

Several other voices echoed the sentiment.

"I'm looking for someone," said Blondie.

"Look somewhere else," said a gravelly voice.

Dakota heard the shuffling of feet suggesting that the sleeping patrons had rallied to drive Blondie out. The place grew quiet again.

In the darkness, he heard Grace scooting toward him.

"They'll be watching the door where we came in," she said.

"Yeah, and probably any obvious second exit." Not wanting to disturb the sleeping patrons, he spoke in a whisper. "And they might try to come back in here once people wake up and wander out."

"I found a piece of metal," she whispered. "Can you take it out of my hand and cut me free?" She turned so her back was to him. He twisted around. His hand brushed over hers and then touched the cold metal.

"I'm afraid I'm going to cut you."

"I'll let you know if you do," she said. "I'll pull my hands as far apart as I can."

His shoulder muscles strained as he bent at an odd angle to touch her wrist and then the rigid plastic of the zip tie. He felt the space where he could cut. Sawing the strong, thin plastic took at least fifteen minutes and he still hadn't freed her.

"I think you made a decent gash. Let me see if I can twist it apart."

He waited, listening to her struggle to break free.

"There—got it," she said. "Let me cut you loose."

Once they were both free, they crawled out from behind the boxes. It was hard to see anything at all. The coughing and snoring told him they needed to move cautiously. Using the flashlight on his phone was out of the question since light seemed to be the only thing that upset the people sleeping in the old building. Calling for help was out of the question too. They needed to preserve their cover.

He pressed close to the wall; Grace was right behind him. They came to the end of the wall without stepping on anyone. He could just make out a stairway about ten feet away. He walked toward it. The stairs were metal and seemed to be fairly sturdy. They moved up them with caution. On the second floor, dusty windows allowed a little more light in than on the first floor. Neon from across the street reflected in the glass.

They moved toward the window that faced the street. The white car was parked several blocks away and Randy paced the sidewalk and watched the building.

They worked their way around to other windows that looked out on an alley. Blondie was leaning on a dumpster, cleaning his fingernails with a pocketknife.

"What do you think?" asked Grace "Should we just wait it out?"

"I doubt they will go away. You heard them—they don't get paid unless we're dead. Once we have daylight and the people in here wake up, they will probably try coming back."

Grace scooted across the floor and picked up a T-shirt. The dirt falling off of it made noise as it scattered on the floor.

"What if we were just a couple of homeless people leaving this building to wander through the city?" She pointed toward some plastic bags in the corner of the room. "Hauling our stuff around."

"That's risky. If they recognize us, they'll come after us."

Grace wandered the floor and picked up a baseball hat that was equally as dirty. "So the trick is not to be recognized." She tossed him the hat. She pulled her hair from the ponytail she usually wore it in and messed it up, so it hung in her eyes. She hunched over and shuffled with a gait that looked nothing like her athletic stride.

"We need to find different tops and bottoms or make these so dirty and torn they're not recognizable."

The sun was just coming up by the time they found enough clothing to create a disguise. Dakota texted Mr. Wilson with an excuse for why they were not at the hotel—by saying that Grace needed to shop for some specialty ingredients. She wanted to be first in line when the shops opened.

They made their way downstairs.

Dakota turned to face her, still talking in a whisper. "We're going to have go out separately and circle the block. Coming out together would be a red flag. When we were upstairs, I saw a flashing sign for an all-night café a block over to the south. Meet outside there. Wait five minutes. If I don't show, keep moving. I'll call you once I'm sure I'm not going to be followed. You do the same for me."

She nodded. "I'll go out first."

They walked toward the door. There was enough light coming through the open door to see a mattress in a corner. A man slept there, his back turned toward them.

She peered out and then pressed herself against the wall. "He's right there watching the door still."

He heard the fear in her voice. "Wait a couple minutes. I'm sure he'll move around and get farther away. He's probably walking around patrolling the area, watching for us" He leaned close to her so he could whisper. They stood face-to-face, their noses almost touching. Feeling a desire to calm her fears, he bent and kissed her gently on the lips then touched his fingers to her cheek. "You'll be all right."

She squeezed his hand. "We're both going to be okay, Dakota." She kissed him and then slipped out into the early-morning light.

His heart beat a little faster from the intensity of the moment. He wanted to hold her in his arms and not let her go. He angled around the open doorway so he could watch her shuffling up the street. Randy continued to watch the doorway while he ambled along the sidewalk across the street.

After a few minutes, Dakota stepped outside and headed in the opposite direction Grace had gone. He squinted as the sun hit his eyes. When he looked up, Randy was on the crosswalk getting ready to come across the street. Dakota's heart squeezed tight. That meant that he would have to walk right past him.

Dakota shuffled along and mumbled to himself. He carried a plastic garbage bag that he and Grace had filled with mostly paper and cardboard. His baseball hat was drawn down over his dirty face.

He could see Randy's feet as they drew closer. There were several other people on the sidewalk. Dakota veered toward the edge of the sidewalk. The two men passed. Dakota kept walking at the same slow pace. He turned his head sideways so he could still see Randy's feet. Randy stopped for a moment, looked around and then kept walking toward the open door of the abandoned building. Randy had clearly sensed something but had not fully processed it.

Dakota kept moving up the street until he got to the

crosswalk. Randy had turned around and was headed back toward him, but he wasn't running. That meant he was acting on suspicion, not a for-sure thing. The smart move for Dakota was to keep moving at the same pace so as not to draw attention to himself.

Dakota crossed the street and headed around the block toward the café. Adrenaline shot through him as Randy drew closer.

As Randy walked toward him, he kept his head down and turned to the side so Randy couldn't get a good look at his face. He shuffled and mumbled to himself.

Though he could not let on, Dakota's heart was pounding. Sweat formed on his forehead.

Randy moved slowly past him.

FIFTEEN

The neon sign for the all-night café flashed up ahead. Grace was within half a block of the rendezvous point when the contact phone from the drug network buzzed in her pocket. Because the plan had gone sideways, she had not had time to toss it as instructed.

She was surprised it was still functional after being in the water at the harbor. She glanced around, not seeing either of the two men. She read the text.

I know where you are.

The number was not Dakota's.

Squashing a rising sense of panic, she glanced all around, still not seeing either man. Some instinct told her to look up. The abandoned building they had been in was several stories higher than any others around it. Blondie stood on the top of the building, looking right at her.

Heart pounding, she turned to look in the opposite direction. Randy was coming directly toward her as he put his phone away. Blondie had texted her to confirm his theory. He had watched her take out her phone right after he texted. He must have let Randy know.

She turned and ran into an alley. When she glanced sideways, Randy had picked up his pace. She kept running. The alley was mostly deserted. Judging from the aroma of spices wafting in the air, the buildings were mostly the back sides of restaurants. She ran past a delivery truck but there were no people around.

Randy was about a block behind her.

She took a side street and then another, hoping to ditch him. The bulkiness of the clothes she wore slowed her down. She'd put on layers to hide her build. When she looked over her shoulder, she didn't see Randy anywhere. But he was probably within less than a minute of catching up with her.

She climbed into a dumpster. Feet pounded past her seconds after she closed the lid. She covered her nose to block out the rotten food smells that surrounded her. She heard footsteps, this time moving more slowly. Probably Randy coming back.

Her phone buzzed. She clenched her teeth.

Now for sure he'd know where she was. She grabbed the first thing she could use as a weapon just as Randy flung open the lid. She tossed a bucket of fish parts on him and then grabbed the next thing her hands found, a container of what was maybe grease and chicken skin. Randy sputtered and stepped back, clawing at his chest as his face grew red with rage. She may have burned him as well.

She slung her legs over, trying to get out of the dumpster. Her feet touched the concrete. Randy had recovered enough to grab her from behind. She kicked him before he had a chance to get her in a stranglehold. He dove for her. She dodged out of the way and took off running through the maze of alleys, trying to find a street where there were people.

She wondered if the text that had enabled Randy to find her was from Dakota or if Randy had texted the phone. She came onto a street where there was a corner grocery. Though it was still closed, people were inside getting ready to open up. There were only a few people on the sidewalk and most of them looked like they were homeless.

Randy came around the corner. A man with a grocery cart shuffled past him and said, "You smell."

Randy brushed his shoulder, maybe trying to get rid of fish particles. She didn't think he would go after her with people around. She stood outside the closed grocery store trying to orient herself.

As Randy closed in on her, she did an about-face and started walking. The man had a gun; she couldn't let him get too close. He'd be able to conceal the gun and control her by pressing it into her back. She pulled her phone out and checked her text. Randy drew closer. She put the phone back in her pocket. She walked a little faster, looking for someplace that was open.

For almost two blocks the man followed her. It was clear he didn't want to draw attention to himself with the few people who were out at this early hour. If he came too close, she might just scream that she was being attacked. Most of the people around this neighborhood probably didn't want to get involved or were too out of it to care, but maybe raising a fuss would be enough to keep him from pulling the gun.

She hurried up the street for one more block before dashing inside a coffee shop that was open. Randy stepped into the shop as well and stood about four feet away from her. Her hands were shaking as she pulled out the phone. The text was from Dakota.

I'm at the café. Where are you?

She glanced up at Randy. His expression was smug.

Randy is watching me. Will get there as soon as I can shake him.

She glanced around and spotted a restroom. She went inside. The restroom had only one stall and a single high small window. She locked the door and jumped up on the sink and tried to dislodge the window. She had only minutes. If she stayed in here too long, Randy would figure out she wasn't using the facilities and start patrolling the outside of the building. The angle at which she had to bend was impossible. If she could even fit through the window, she was going to end up tumbling headfirst onto the street.

Someone knocked on the door and then jiggled the handle.

"I'll be out in just a minute."

No one answered back. She feared it was Randy. The restroom was in a hallway that had several doors—the men's bathroom, an employee's-only door and a door that was probably a janitor's closet.

If he was waiting outside the door and no one was in the hallway, he could grab her. It had been a mistake to enter the restroom.

Her phone dinged. It was Dakota.

Where are you?

At the Good Morning coffee shop. Trapped in the women's restroom. I'm afraid he's waiting outside for me. Should have thought this through.

Hold tight. I'll come to you.

She pressed the phone against her chest as a sense of relief flooded through her. Dakota would come for her. She saw that now. Not just when she was in physical danger. He was a different man than he was three years ago.

There was another knock on the door. "Ma'am, are you okay in there?" The voice was female.

"I'm sorry. Give me a second. I'm a little bit sick. Would you wait and help me find a seat?"

"Sure, honey," said the woman.

Grace unlocked and opened the door. Sure enough, Randy was waiting for her a few feet away.

The woman who had spoken to her wore a coffee-shop apron. She was older, with blond-and-white hair and half glasses. The woman gestured toward Randy. "Your husband was worried about you."

Randy stepped toward her. "I'll take it from here."

Fear charged through Grace like a herd of elephants. "You know, I think I just need to sit down."

As she pushed past Randy, he reached out and grabbed her arm just above the elbow. "Let me help you." He squeezed her arm tight enough to make the nerve endings hurt.

The older employee tried to slip past them.

Grace yanked away. "I'm all right." The noise of the busy coffee shop around the corner reached her. "I just need to sit down." She reached out for the older woman and whispered in her ear. "Please, help me. That man is not my husband."

With a backward glance at Randy, the older woman raised her voice. "Sure, honey, let me get you to a seat."

She escorted Grace to a booth by the door and patted her shoulder. "You just sit down and take it easy. Do I need to call the police?"

"That would be good."

Randy ambled through the coffee shop toward her. The older woman shot him a glance filled with daggers which made him stutter in his step. He must have picked up that Grace had said something about him to the barista. Or at least he suspected something was up. Randy stopped and took a seat one booth away from Grace, narrowing his eyes at her. The blond barista had disappeared into the back of the coffee shop probably to make the call to the police.

At best, the police would only be able to detain Randy long enough to question him, but it might be enough for her and Dakota to get away.

The coffee shop had gotten even more crowded from the time she'd entered it.

Dakota burst through the door and looked around. Several people blocked his view of the booth. Grace got to her feet and pushed through the crowd. Dakota wrapped her in his arms and whispered, "I've got you. You're safe now."

"I know," she said.

Dakota held on to Grace as they stepped out into the early-morning sunlight. He'd seen Randy in the coffee shop, and he had no doubt that they would be followed.

As long as there were people around, he doubted either man would try something.

The city was starting to wake up and get busier. Traffic had increased.

He squeezed Grace's shoulder. "You okay?"

"I don't know if it's because I'm tired or what, but I wasn't making good decisions back there."

Randy stepped outside when they had gone less than half a block.

A police car pulled to the curb as they made their way up the street.

"One of the baristas called the police on Randy," she said. "It buys us some time."

They walked at least ten blocks. Dakota didn't see any sign of Blondie or Randy.

He pointed up ahead at a food truck that advertised breakfast burritos. "I'm sure your decision-making ability was affected by hunger."

They ordered their burritos and kept walking, glancing over their shoulders frequently.

Dakota took several bites of his burrito. "Given what happened, I think we need to make contact with Henry and Elise and evaluate where we're at."

"You mean pull the plug on the investigation?" She took several more bites of her food. "I know we were set up, but I feel like we have a degree of trust with Mr. Wilson and his family that might open some doors. We need to get back there. I don't know why we were set up. Somebody has been gunning for us almost from the beginning."

"While I was waiting for you in the café, Mr. Wilson called and wanted to know where I was. I made an excuse that you'd had a medical issue and we were at the ER."

"So you bought us a little bit of time," she said.

"The interesting thing was that Mr. Wilson said his wife and son had decided to join them."

"So they might be involved in some way. Though they can probably run this operation from Montana. They seem to favor hiring thugs to do their dirty work."

"We still don't know what happened to Cory," said Dakota.

"Maybe Justin is telling the truth and he's in rehab."

"I just think we need perspective on the investigation. See if we can put some of the puzzle pieces in place," he said.

She took the last bite of her burrito. "Is it possible that someone has wanted us dead from the beginning?"

Dakota shrugged. "The trouble started after you made contact with Cory and implied that you wanted in on the action." When he looked over his shoulder, Dakota noticed Blondie leaning against a building, watching them. "We got company—behind you."

Grace didn't turn around and look. "Which one?"

"The blond guy." Dakota scanned the city streets. "That other guy is probably around here too."

"Okay, I guess you can phone it in," she said. "Have them bring a car that doesn't draw attention to pick us up. I just think if we stay away too long, we'll lose the trust we've built with the Wilsons. It just feels like something might break there soon."

"It makes sense to try to keep that door open." He pulled out his phone and made the call. He clicked off. "It's all set. Blue sedan will meet us at the intersection of First Avenue and Pine, about a ten-minute walk from here."

"That's close to Pike Place market."

"It will be busy. Us being picked up won't draw attention," said Dakota. "Assuming our friends will be following us."

"We have to assume that, right?" she said.

They continued to walk. Grace reached out and took his hand. He remembered the brief kisses they'd shared back at the abandoned building. When all this was over, maybe they could have a talk about trying to date.

Pike Place was bustling with activity. Buskers and men yelling and throwing fish to entertain the shoppers. He could smell the salt air as they pushed through the crowd toward the rendezvous point.

A crowd surrounded them. Grace had let go of his hand and people had moved in between them. He lost sight of her for just a moment.

He felt a sudden stinging pain on his left shoulder. Someone had cut him with a knife and then slipped back into the crowd. Though he did not see them in the crowd, one of the two men must have cut him. He grabbed his arm where the blood was spreading across the fabric of his shirt. Where had Grace gone?

Fear nearly paralyzed him as he put pressure on his wound and squeezed through the crowd searching for her. What if they had cut him as a distraction so the other man could grab Grace?

He leaned forward, breathing through the stinging pain and feeling himself getting nauseous His vision blurred as he scanned each face. He thought he saw the blond man headed toward the waterfront. He moved in that direction.

The man he thought was Blondie turned sideways. He'd been mistaken. His body was going into shock.

"Dakota, what happened?" Grace was beside him.

"I was cut." He looked into her soft eyes. "Did they come after you?"

She shook her head. "Let's get up to the rendezvous point. You need medical attention fast."

She positioned herself by his good shoulder and wrapped an arm around his waist. They made their way up to the street.

"I was afraid they'd grabbed you." He was blubbering because of the shock and blood loss. "I don't know what I would do without my Gracie. I care about you so much."

The car sent for them pulled to the curb. She opened the door and helped him into the back seat and then ran around to the other side of the car and got in beside him.

"Hang in there, Dakota. We're almost to a safe place."

He hoped that was true. The blood and the pain made it hard for him to think clearly.

"We better make a detour to the ER," she told the agent.

Her voice seemed to be fading. He could feel himself losing consciousness.

SIXTEEN

Grace clamped her hand on Dakota's cut as he slumped forward and let the hand he'd been applying pressure with hang limp. He looked as white as rice and as if he might pass out from blood loss.

Their driver was a younger agent whom Grace recognized from the shooting range but she did not know his name.

The man sped up. "Hang in there. I know a fast way to the ER."

Buildings and street signs flashed by in her peripheral vision as she focused on Dakota. He was still conscious, but it was clear he was in shock.

"Stay with me, Dakota." She rested her hand on his cheek.

He lifted his chin slightly. The cut must have been deep. His shirt was soaked with blood.

The young agent pulled up to the emergency room entrance. He jumped out and helped Grace get Dakota out of the car.

"I'll take it from here. If you want to find a parking space," she said.

"Okay, sure," said the agent.

Once they were inside, the woman behind the check-in desk took one look at them and came around the desk to help. "Looks like we need to take you right back to a room. We'll deal with the paperwork later."

She left them in an exam room with a curtain for a wall. A nurse made an appearance right away, got an IV with painkillers going and cut away the bloody fabric. Both Grace and the nurse winced when they saw the cut.

"I'll get the doctor in here right away."

Within minutes the doctor showed up to deal with the wound. Dakota closed his eyes while the cut was disinfected and stitched up. Grace gripped the railing of the hospital bed, hardly able to breathe.

The doctor spoke to her while he focused on taking care of Dakota's injury. "Are you his wife?"

"I used to be," she said. "We work together."

"That's always nice to see," said the doctor. "That you are able to get along despite past differences."

Dakota opened his eyes. His gaze fell on Grace. Even in the mental haze caused by the blood loss and medication, the look he gave her made her heart flutter.

"Let him rest for as long as he needs. I'll sign the discharge papers and send him home with a prescription. They'll be at the front desk."

Grace thanked the doctor.

"We should get going, huh?" Dakota's eyes were half-closed and he had to take a breath between each word.

She stroked his forehead. "Why don't you do what the doctor said and sleep. It won't matter if we're a couple hours late."

"I like that," said Dakota. His voice was a bit listless.

"Like what?" She leaned over him.

He reached up and rested his fingers on her chin, offering her a soft smile. "You being close to me."

The painkillers had loosened his tongue.

"I like it too," she said and kissed his forehead.

She phoned the agent who'd driven them here to let him know what was happening, and he said he'd wait. Forty-five minutes later, Dakota was awake and felt well enough to walk. They got into the car, both of them in the back seat again.

As they sat side by side, Dakota's hand found hers. They rolled through the city.

The agent checked his rearview mirror.

Grace sat up a little straighter. "Something wrong?"

"That white car has been behind us every time I check my mirror."

Her throat tightened. "It's the men who are after us."

The agent wove through traffic. He took a turn so sharply that Grace and Dakota swayed one way and then the other.

"Sorry, didn't mean to hurt you more," said the agent.

"Do what you've got to do," said Dakota.

The agent turned into a large parking lot and found a parking space. "We can wait him out. Hopefully, he'll drive past."

Grace looked through the back window, half expecting to see the white car charging toward them. They waited a full ten minutes.

Dakota rested his head against the back seat. "I don't think we should go to headquarters, just in case we're followed."

"Can we make arrangements to meet Henry and Elise somewhere else?"

"I can get on the phone," said the agent.

Grace closed her eyes and listened to the conversation. They would meet at the Marriott down by the harbor. There was a comic-book convention going on, so lots of people to serve as a distraction if they were followed.

The agent hung up and turned sideways. "So you guys are to check in to room 512 and wait to hear from Henry and Elise. Don't leave the room," said the agent.

The agent pulled out of the parking space, rolled through the parking lot and back into traffic. The rest of the drive was uneventful. The agent arrived at the hotel check-in area.

Grace leaned forward and patted his shoulder. "Thanks for everything. You did good."

As they got out of the car, she looked down. They were both still dressed in their homeless clothes.

Dakota leaned on her for support. "I don't think it matters what we look like as long as we can pay."

"You're probably right?"

The lobby was teeming with people, many of them dressed in costumes. She recognized some of them from games and comic books and movies.

After buying some clean clothes in the gift shop, they took the elevator to the fifth floor. Once they were in the room, they took turns showering and changing into fresh clothes. They both collapsed on the bed on top of the covers and fell asleep.

When Grace woke up and pulled the curtain back, the gray of the sky indicated it was early evening. They had slept through the day. Her stomach growled. Dakota still slept.

She ordered room service and then checked Dakota's

phone to see if maybe they had slept through a phone call. No word from Henry or Elise, but Mr. Wilson had called wanting to know how things were going. She texted back that they were still at the hospital.

Room service arrived. Burgers, fries and milkshakes. Dakota opened his eyes. "That smells delicious."

She clicked on the television and found a trivia game show. "You always beat me at this game, remember?"

They ate at the table. In between bites, Dakota answered questions on the game show. When the commercial came on, he lowered the volume and set his burger down. "Feels like old times in some weird way."

Eating dinner with him had felt cozy and familiar. Despite the intensity of all they had been through, they found this small oasis. "It's nice to be here with you."

Dakota's phone rang. He pushed back his chair and walked across the room to pick it up. Though she heard only one side of the conversation, it was clear he was talking to either Henry or Elise. He clicked off the phone. "Elise can't get here until tomorrow morning. She wants us to stay in the room for our safety. She'll call when she's outside the door."

"Just Elise, not Henry?"

Dakota shrugged.

"Can you call Mr. Wilson and make some excuse as to why we're still not there?"

"Sure."

Dakota made the call. She was grateful for the opportunity to rest. She watched some television and went to bed.

Once morning came, she pulled the curtain back and looked out the window. There were so many people wandering around dressed in costumes that anyone not in a costume stood out.

She zeroed in on a blond man. Her heart raced. "How did he find us?"

Dakota came out of the bathroom where he'd been showering. "Something wrong?"

"One of our friends is here."

Dakota hurried across the room and pulled back the curtain a couple of inches. "If he's here, I bet you his partner is around too."

"Do you think they'll be able to find out what room we're in?"

"We're registered under Deleray, but they would have to be pretty savvy to get that information about our room number." Dakota retrieved his phone. "Come on, I have an idea. Get that phone. You wait back by the vending machine—it's a little room where you can peek out without people seeing you. Anyone coming up the stairs will have to walk past there. I'll keep an eye on the elevators. Elise must be on her way."

Heart pounding, she picked up her phone. "Good plan. Let's go then."

They both rushed toward the door. He grabbed her and pulled her close. His lips covered hers. As he held and kissed her, she felt herself melting against him. It did feel like old times in so many ways.

He pulled away and gazed down at her. His eyes filled with warmth, his expression glowing with affection. "I know that you can handle yourself. But I wish we didn't have to split up."

His kiss had taken her breath and her words away. She could only manage a nod.

Dakota yanked open the door. He cupped his shoulder, wincing. His shoulder must have still been hurting him. They stepped outside onto the carpeted hallway. Several people milled through the hallway or stood at doors with their key cards.

If Blondie managed to get their room number, it would probably take him less than ten minutes to get up to the fifth floor.

She and Dakota split off in opposite directions. She gave a backward glance toward Dakota and prayed that they would both be safe and together soon.

Dakota walked briskly toward the elevators and positioned himself behind a wall so he could see who had gotten off the elevator once they stepped into the hall. Unless they turned around, they weren't likely to see him. There were no hotel rooms on the other side of where he was hiding. He pressed against the wall.

The elevator dinged. A moment later, several people, two of them laughing and holding hands, headed up the hallway.

He waited, paced a little and then got back into position.

His phone dinged. A text from Grace.

Blondie just walked past me.

Before he could click off his phone, another text came through. This one from Elise's number.

Standing outside your door. Safe to open.

Dakota could feel all the air suction out of his lungs as a realization spread through him. He hurried down the hall toward room 512. Blondie looked up from the phone he was holding. Elise was not there. Somehow Elise was involved in all this; she must have hired Blondie and Randy.

Blondie's eyes grew wide at the sight of Dakota. Dakota raced toward the elevator. Two women were in the sitting area outside the elevator. Dakota pushed the elevator button. Blondie slowed when he saw the two people sitting in the chairs.

He came and stood beside Dakota. His voice filled with menace, he said, "Going down, are you?"

"Doing what I got to do." He couldn't get on an elevator alone with this man.

"We're going down too," said one of the women in the chairs.

The door slid open. "After you, ladies." Dakota waited until the women got on before stepping into the elevator. Blondie wedged himself in.

One of the women turned toward Blondie. "Aren't you hot in that jacket?"

"I'm fine," said Blondie.

Dakota knew he wore the jacket to conceal his gun. The numbers raced by. Dakota took out his phone to text Grace.

Meet me in the lobby. Elise is involved. Her henchmen are here.

Elise might even be in the hotel. Either Elise had texted the lie that she was outside their room or Blondie had ended up with her phone and had done it himself. There was little chance the thugs could have spotted Elise in the hotel, randomly figured she was an agent and ambushed her, so Dakota was almost certain she was in on all this. The elevator doors opened up and Dakota rushed out. The lobby was teeming with people. Blondie stayed at his heels. Randy was most likely around here somewhere. He needed to make sure Grace was safe.

Grace had probably taken the stairs since she was closest to them. He pulled his phone out.

Get out on the next floor and take the elevator to the lobby.

Got it.

Text when you're about to arrive.

Got it. On floor three now.

He held the phone in his hand while he wandered around scanning the crowd. Blondie stayed close. Another text came in from Grace.

Almost there.

Dakota did an about-face and headed toward the elevators. A crowd of people in costumes swarmed toward him. He was like a fish swimming upstream squeezing past people. He could see the elevators. When he peered over his shoulder, Blondie had been swallowed up by the crowd.

The doors opened. He pushed past more people.

An older woman stepped out. And then Grace was there looking around.

Off to his side, he spotted Randy, who was making a beeline toward the elevators. Grace locked eyes with Dakota. She stepped toward him.

The crowd thinned, allowing Dakota to run toward Grace. Randy reached her first.

Grace spotted him, turned and pushed Randy. "Stop following me. I'm going to call hotel security."

The crowd glared at Randy.

"This man is stalking me," she said loudly. "I'm getting hotel security right now." She headed toward Dakota.

Dakota had to hand it to her. Grace could think on her feet. She wrapped her arm through his.

"Blondie at ten o'clock," she said.

The blond man had positioned himself by the hotel entrance. They wouldn't be able to leave without him right on their tail. They had no car to escape in.

Randy hung back but was clearly tracking them.

They headed toward the first open door they found, a ballroom where the convention merchandise was being sold. Dakota scanned the room, feeling a rising tension in his muscles. There was no second exit. Randy stood just outside the door.

They had to find a different way to escape.

SEVENTEEN

The ballroom was wall-to-wall with people and merchandisers who sold everything from comic books to T-shirts to stuffed animals to costume accessories.

Grace held on to Dakota's hand.

"I don't see either one of them. Do you?"

"Blondie is probably still watching the entrance. The other guy is right outside the only exit to the ballroom," said Dakota.

An idea came into her head. It had worked once before. She stepped toward a merchant who sold capes. "I'll take the blue one." She paid the man. She turned to face Dakota with a quick glance around, not seeing either of the men. She handed Dakota the cape. "Put it on."

"Good thinking," said Dakota. "Disguises."

She glanced around at the crowd before moving to a booth that sold masks that a great deal of the patrons were wearing. The mask was a sort of ventilator with goggles that concealed their entire face. By the time they'd moved through the ballroom, she'd found a military-style coat for herself.

As they made their way around, she spotted Randy

by the entrance of the ballroom. She didn't need to explain the plan to Dakota. There was only one way out of the ballroom.

They lingered, pretending to look at some stuffed animals. Dakota squeezed her hand. At least ten people were headed toward the entrance. They hurried across the carpet, melting into the crowd of people leaving and entering the ballroom. She could see Randy out of the corner of her eye as he paced, pretended to look at merchandise and glanced around.

Sweat trickled down her back. She let go of Dakota's hand. Knowing that Randy was looking for a couple, they had to walk out separately. The mask made her face hot and the goggles were made of a poor-quality plastic that distorted her view. As she peered through them, out of focus people moved past her.

She stepped through the ballroom entrance, not seeing Dakota. Though she spotted several people with the same blue cape.

Dakota was right beside her. It was impossible to talk with the masks on.

They ambled toward the lobby entrance. Blondie was seated, but his body language suggested he was still taking note of everyone who walked through the lobby.

Dakota led her back toward the checkout counter and then down a hallway. He lifted the mask and wiped the sweat from his brow. "There has got to be another way out of here. We can't hope to pull this off a third time."

They hurried down the hallway. The sound of pots and pans banging and sizzling along with the aroma of spices reached them.

"Maybe through the kitchen," she said.

Both of them pulled their masks off as they entered

the bustling kitchen. As they wove around the counters, a few people stared at them, but most were too busy loading plates, barking orders and watching the grill to ask why they wandered through.

Dakota pushed open the door and stepped out onto a loading dock. Several trucks were parked outside.

Grace took in a deep breath of cool spring air. "What do we do now?"

"Let's grab a taxi and get back to the parking garage where we left the rental. Elise is involved in this somehow," he added, explaining the text that had come from her indicating it was safe to open up when it was Blondie standing outside their door. "I think we should try to meet with Henry face-to-face, but first we need to get back to the Wilsons. This investigation must tie back to them somehow. Maybe we were getting too close to the guilty party and Elise for whatever reason called out all the stops."

She tensed. Taxi pickup would involve having to go to the front of the hotel. "There might be a taxi waiting. I don't think we should stand out in the open even with the masks on."

"Let's go check."

They hurried to the side of the hotel and peered out. Two taxis were parked in the circular driveway. They might be waiting for people who had phoned for a taxi and they might be hoping to pick up a fare.

"Stay here," said Dakota.

He didn't give her time to protest. He wouldn't be able to speak to the taxi driver with his mask on. The hotel lobby had two large windows that looked out on the drop-off area. She watched Dakota approach the first taxi. She stepped out and craned her neck. Blondie was still sitting with his back to the window. It was just a matter of time before Randy figured out they had slipped out the ballroom and he and then Blondie would start searching the hotel and beyond.

Dakota leaned into the first taxi and spoke to the driver for a moment, but then stepped back and walked toward the second. He approached the second taxi and repeated his actions. This time he signaled for Grace to come over.

He opened the back door and waited for her. Grace surveyed the area around her and then glanced back toward the lobby. Though her heart beat wildly, she walked at a pace that would not draw attention to her.

A valet driver pulled up into the driveway with a compact car. Elise emerged from the hotel. Grace ducked down behind the open door. Dakota had already gotten in the taxi.

"Change of plans." She pointed at the car just as Elise tipped the valet driver and got in. "Follow that car."

"What is this about?" asked the taxi driver.

"There is a hundred bucks in it for you if you do," said Dakota.

The taxi driver, who looked like she was college age, shrugged. "Okay, I could use the money."

As they pulled away from the hotel, Grace glanced toward the lobby. Blondie was no longer sitting with his back to the window. She turned and stared out the back window of the taxi just as Blondie stepped outside. She did not have time to duck out of view before recognition spread across his face. Now Blondie knew they were leaving. Their taxi picked up speed and headed toward the street.

* * *

Though the taxi driver did a pretty good job of keeping up with Elise's car, Dakota found himself wishing he was behind the wheel. Twice they had almost lost her on the expressway.

Even if Blondie was communicating with Elise, the yellow cab did provide a degree of cover. When he looked around at the other cars, he always spotted at least one other yellow cab. He didn't see the white car anywhere either.

Elise switched lanes twice.

Grace touched his arm. "Do you think we should call Henry?"

"I suppose. Do you think you can trust him?" He handed her his phone.

"I can't see a man like Henry involved in something like this. I've known him since I was a rookie."

"Okay, I'll trust your judgement. Do you want to make the call?" He wanted to keep an eye on Elise just in case the taxi driver lost her.

Grace took the phone and clicked in the number. All the essential numbers they needed to know they'd memorized. If the phone fell into the wrong hands while they were undercover, it had to look like they were who they claimed they were.

Grace held the phone to her ear. "Henry…it's Grace."

Dakota kept his eye on the cars in front of him and half listened to the one-sided conversation as Grace explained the situation and their suspicions about Elise. Henry said something and then there was a long pause before Grace responded.

The mood had shifted so significantly that Dakota pulled his focus away from the traffic. Grace's jaw stiffened. She shook her head. "Henry, you know I wouldn't do something like that."

Henry said something.

Grace seemed to be getting more upset. "It's Elise… not me."

She hung up.

The look on Grace's face was enough to make Dakota's throat go tight. "What's wrong?" He was afraid to ask.

"It sounds like Elise has put some effort into poisoning the department's view of us. I don't know if she has written false reports or what, but Henry seems to think we've entered the drug trade—that we've gone over to the other side."

Dakota's hand curled into a fist as a sense of outrage and a desire for justice filled him. He glanced up ahead as the taxi switched lanes. Elise was signaling that she was taking an exit ramp. "We've got to figure out what Elise is up to and clear our names. If we had some evidence, we could show Henry."

Grace nodded, then she leaned forward to speak to the taxi driver. "As soon as she stops, go past by a few blocks and let us out." She pulled out a credit card. "We need to pay you now. Add the hundred to the charge."

The taxi driver took the card and ran it through her machine while she kept her eyes on the road.

Elise slowed down as she turned onto a street lined with boutique businesses and restaurants. She slipped into a parking space.

"Go around the block," said Dakota. "Not too far."

Both of them looked through the back window as Elise got out of her car.

"Slow down a little," said Grace. "We need to see where she's going."

"You're in luck," said the taxi driver as she pressed the brakes. "We just hit a red light."

Elise walked half a block and then stepped into an art gallery. This could be a total dead end. Maybe Blondie hadn't communicated with Elise or hadn't seen her leaving. Elise had not shown any awareness that she knew she was being followed.

Dakota undid the cape he'd been wearing while Grace slipped out of the military jacket that would only attract attention now that they were away from the hotel.

The light turned green and the driver turned at the next intersection and let them out.

"You forgot your costume stuff."

"Keep it as a souvenir," said Dakota.

As he slammed the door, he heard the taxi driver say, "Thanks for making my day interesting."

They hurried up the sidewalk. The art gallery had only one large window. He didn't see Elise, though it looked like the gallery had other rooms. He saw one older man with a cane examining a large sculpture that hung from the ceiling and took up most of the floor space. There was no one behind the counter by the door.

Dakota took in a deep breath. "Well, we're either walking into a trap or a confrontation."

Grace nodded.

They stepped into the first room of the gallery. Besides the giant sculpture that looked like a spiral staircase made of colorful paper, there were paintings and three-dimensional art hung on the wall.

Their footsteps seemed to echo as they stepped through the silent gallery. The small room opened up into a much larger room with a high ceiling. L-shaped partitions were set up displaying black-and-white photographs close to the door. More sculptures were scattered through the remaining area of the space and paintings hung on all three walls.

Four people mingled through the displays, none of them Elise. There was another door that looked like it might lead down a hallway. From where he stood, Dakota saw several doors. Maybe where classrooms were or artworks were stored.

Elise emerged from the hallway. She'd probably been in the restroom. Both of them ducked behind a photo display. They circled around to have a better view. Elise seemed profoundly interested in a painting on the far wall. Her back remained to them.

One of the other patrons, a man, eased toward her, stopping to look at several paintings before coming to stand by Elise. The man wore a hat. It took Dakota a second to process what he was seeing. Justin Wilson. It was his stride and demeanor more so than a clear view of his face that had clued Dakota in.

Elise and Justin spoke with their heads close together while they pretended to be admiring the art. Their body language suggested romantic involvement. The revelation of what he was seeing sunk in slowly. So maybe this trip to Seattle had been a setup from the start to get rid of Grace. Elise had displayed some reluctance about them going to Montana. Being in Mr. Wilson's household meant he and Grace would be getting too close to the truth. Elise may have been the one who arranged for the men to try to take them out at the cabin and the other times as well.

"I have to get a picture of them together," said Dakota. "It's the only thing that will clear us."

"Careful," whispered Grace.

Dakota moved toward a partition that was closer to where Justin and Elise were talking. Justin moved down to another painting and Elise followed him seconds later. They continued to talk at a low volume and stare at the painting.

Dakota waited for the moment when they turned sideways so he could at least capture their faces in profile. The partitions were high enough that only Dakota's head down to his nose was visible. If he bent his head like he was studying a photograph, he wasn't visible at all. He'd have to rest the phone on the rim of the partition. Grace eased over to a different partition and pulled out her phone as well. He clenched his jaw. He had a shot of Elise, but Justin's hat was still pulled low on his face and he turned toward the painting.

The old man with the cane who had been in the other room entered the larger space. Two other patrons, a teenager and a woman who might have been her mom, were looking at a display tucked away in a corner. The last person, an older woman, had gone down the hallway.

Not wanting to draw attention to himself, Dakota moved to another partition. This one gave him a view of Justin, but Elise was turned so her face wasn't showing.

Elise glanced in his direction. He crouched down behind the display. When he glanced over at Grace, she was shaking her head. They'd been spotted. They headed toward the door through the smaller room and out onto the street.

Dakota didn't look back until they were halfway up

the block. Elise stepped out onto the sidewalk with a phone in her hands. Her goons must be close by.

"We're not going to get away on foot." Grace spoke between breaths as both of them broke into a jog.

He glanced around. They had turned up an alley that only had the backs of businesses with employees-only doors or no entrances at all. They needed to get to the storefronts and find a shop to hide in before they were spotted.

Both of them sprinted toward a street with lots of traffic.

Blondie appeared at one end of the alley. He raised his gun. He was within shooting range. Dakota doubted anyone would hear the gunshot in the alley. If they did, they'd think it was a car backfiring.

They turned and ran the other way.

Randy appeared at the other end of the alley, stalking toward them to get within range.

They were trapped.

EIGHTEEN

As both men drew closer, Grace dashed toward one of the back-alley doors. Locked. Dakota sprinted toward a fire escape and started to climb up. She ran to where he was.

Blondie raised his pistol and fired. The shot pinged off the metal of the fire escape.

She pressed against the wall. Dakota raced up the ladder.

Randy stalked toward them and Blondie raised the gun again. This time he was close enough that he wouldn't miss. Her heart pounded as adrenaline-fueled panic raged through her body.

A door burst open and a man carrying a cardboard box headed toward the dumpster. Both Randy and Blondie hid their guns. Randy turned his back like he was headed up the alley. The man threw the box in the dumpster, stared at Blondie and Grace for just a moment, and then whistled nervously.

Grace took advantage of the disruption and hurried up the ladder after Dakota as the whistling man went back into the building he'd come out of. When she looked down, Blondie was coming up after them.

The rooftop had a container garden and a cage where pigeons were kept. That meant there had to be a way down. Dakota and Grace ran toward what looked like a tiny building with a door. That had to be how people got up. She prayed the door wasn't locked.

Blondie emerged at the top of the fire escape and stepped out onto the roof, heading toward them.

They got to the door. It swung open. They hurried down a narrow creaking stairway. Dakota pushed open a door. They were back out on a street that had more art galleries and shops that catered to tourists.

He grabbed Grace's hand and slipped into the first shop that had an open sign flashing. The shop signs indicated that it was an import shop where everything from the fabric to the furniture came from Japan. A man who was barely out of his teens stood behind the counter flipping through a magazine. He looked surprised when Grace and Dakota entered.

"Can I help you?"

Grace glanced toward the storefront where Blondie paced and pulled out his phone.

"Is there a back way out of here?" They had to escape before Randy could move into place.

The store clerk pointed as his forehead furrowed. Something about their demeanor must have suggested they didn't have time to explain. They ran through a storage room and pushed the door. Once again, they were in an alley where there wasn't any foot traffic. Though he was a block away, Randy bolted toward them.

They shot up the alley toward another street. She could smell salt air. They must be close to the water. Randy was getting closer. They hurried down stairs into a restaurant that looked out on the harbor. The bell attached to the door chimed as they entered. There were only four tables and no sign of a waitstaff; noises emanated from behind a screen where the kitchen must have been.

"We need to call someone to come and get us." Dakota took a seat in a booth and she sat opposite him.

The bell above the door dinged and Blondie came in. Randy must be outside. A man with an apron around his waist emerged from behind the screen. He looked at Blondie. "Have a seat. I'll be with you in just a moment." He walked over to Dakota and Grace.

Blondie chose the table that provided him with a view of Grace and Dakota and the only door out.

The waiter stepped toward where Grace and Dakota were seated. "Sorry I didn't come out right away. My hands were full when I heard the bell the first time. What can I get you two to drink?" He handed them each a menu.

"We'll just have coffee for now," said Dakota.

The waiter brought a menu over to Blondie as well and asked him what he would like to drink.

Blondie glared at Grace, a look so filled with rage that it caused her breath to catch in her throat.

Blondie didn't look at the waiter. "Just bring me some water."

"Certainly, sir." The waiter's tone suggested he was a bit guarded toward Blondie's thinly veiled animosity.

The waiter disappeared into the back room.

"You're not going to get away," said Blondie, his voice filled with venom as he offered them a toothy grin.

Neither of them responded, though Grace felt her

cheeks getting hot. Through the window she could see Randy pacing on the wooden walkway that surrounded the little restaurant.

Dakota took out his phone and typed.

A second later her phone pinged. She took it out of her pocket.

I have a friend who lives half an hour from here. Do you know anyone who could get here faster? It can't be anyone connected to the DEA.

She shook her head.

Dakota typed some more on his phone, sending a text to his friend.

The waiter brought their coffee. He left and returned to sit the water down in front of Blondie.

"Did you have a chance to look at the menu?"

"I'm not hungry," said Blondie.

"Sir, if you're going to sit in our establishment, I need to ask that you order something."

Blondie tossed the menu to one side. "Fine, I'll have coffee too."

"All righty then."

Blondie pulled his phone out and texted. She half expected her phone to ding and get a threatening text, but it didn't.

She had a feeling Blondie might be alerting Elise with information about where they were so reinforcements could be brought in.

Even once help arrived, it would be a challenge to get out to the friend's car and get away. This was going to be one of the longest half hours of her life.

* * *

As they waited, Dakota felt like a noose was tightening around his neck. After he got in touch with his friend John from the Coast Guard, he texted Grace again while Blondie narrowed his eyes at them and took a sip of coffee.

My friend will be coming by boat. He'll let us know when he's in the harbor.

Grace nodded.

Escaping by boat seemed the smart thing to do since Randy would be patrolling the street and the entrance. A half hour was a lot of time for Blondie to call in more help in taking them out. He had the feeling getting down to the harbor would be like running the gauntlet.

They both had another cup of coffee. Feeling like they ought to buy something more while they occupied a table for so long, they also ordered cinnamon rolls, which turned out to be the size of Frisbees. While they consumed the delicious pastries, boats came in to the harbor and docked. Randy disappeared and then returned about ten minutes later to stand on the balcony that faced the harbor.

Providing his friend hadn't been delayed in any way, they still had ten minutes to wait.

If Blondie would leave the restaurant, they could slip out through the kitchen, but it didn't look like that was going to happen. Blondie sipped his coffee and glared at them.

The waiter came and stood by Blondie's table so his view of Grace and Dakota was blocked.

The waiter didn't hide his irritation from his voice. "Sir, I'm going to have to ask that you order something besides coffee."

"You don't look that busy."

While his view was blocked, Dakota took advantage of the moment. He and Grace bolted toward the kitchen and out the back door.

When they stepped out onto the sand, salt air and the sound of gulls greeted them. To Dakota's relief, Randy was not standing on the balcony that faced the waterfront. They hurried down to the harbor, their shoes making crunching noises on the sand.

They slipped behind a storage hut. Dakota peered out. Blondie was making his way toward them. He must not have been able to follow them through the kitchen. Being rude to waiters was never a good idea.

"Let's keep moving," Dakota said. He studied his surroundings. There was a shop that rented Jet Skis, but it looked like no one was around.

"There." Grace pointed. A group of people gathered at the shore, probably tourists waiting to board a boat. They hurried toward the crowd and slipped into the middle of them. The tourists turned their attention to a large cruise ship that was offshore but moving toward the harbor.

They had maybe five minutes before the boat docked. Blondie wandered the shoreline. He hadn't spotted them yet.

The boat came into shore and lowered a ladder. The crowd moved toward it. Grace and Dakota stayed in the middle of the cluster. People chatted excitedly about what they were going to see. There were maybe fifty people. No one seemed to mind that they were not part of the initial group. They must have thought that Grace and Dakota were just latecomers to the tour.

The crowd moved as a unit toward the boat but then boarded one by one. On deck, the captain of the boat greeted them while another man held a hand out to help them up. As the crowd thinned, Grace and Dakota moved toward the back of the remaining group of people.

Blondie had detoured to check around the closed Jet Ski shop but now was searching the shoreline.

Only fifteen or so people were left to board the ship. Dakota tugged on her sleeve and they took off down the shore, walking briskly. Running would too quickly draw attention. There were a dozen or so people on the shore enjoying the day or preparing to get on boats.

Dakota gazed toward open water, hoping to see John's small craft.

Grace's fear-filled voice reached his ears. "Blondie's seen us. He's coming our way."

Blondie jogged toward them.

Dakota gazed up ahead. The area where the boats came in to dock ended in forty feet and beyond that was open beach, where several people were flying kites. "Just stay where people can see us. He's not going to pull a gun with witnesses around."

Dakota hoped that wouldn't change now. The problem was there were just not that many people around. There was a danger that Blondie might be able to get close enough to shoot them point-blank and then slip away in the ensuing panic.

NINETEEN

As Blondie drew closer to them, Grace tried to quell the rising sense of being trapped. The people on the cruise ship had boarded and the boat was backing out of the dock. Several of the people who had been on the shore had boarded boats or walked away from the shore.

The people flying the kites had moved down the shore as well.

"Your friend should be here by now," she said.

"I know. Something must have delayed him," said Dakota. "Let's stay close to the water. Someone is bound to come out on the deck of their boat."

Her heart squeezed tight. That meant moving toward Blondie. "Okay."

They walked close to the shore. Blondie stopped and watched them. Randy made an appearance as well, blocking the possibility of going back to the little restaurant and the shops that surrounded it.

"They don't know that we're going to get away by boat. I suppose that works in our favor." She dared not look out at the arriving boats, fearing that might give their escape plan away.

They walked along the beach. They passed by

Blondie who was forty feet away. He took several steps toward them but then stopped. She followed the line of his gaze, hearing voices off to the side. A man and a woman had come up on the deck of a boat.

Dakota tugged at her elbow. "He's here."

There were several open areas scattered along the pier where John could come into dock.

They kept walking.

Blondie and Randy both drew closer to them.

The sound of the approaching boat grew louder. Then stopped.

Dakota turned around. His friend had come to shore behind them, closer to where the kite flyers were. They jogged down shore. John smiled and waved at them.

Blondie moved toward them but then stopped and pulled out his phone.

Grace and Dakota sprinted toward the boat.

"Boy, are we glad to see you," said Dakota. "We got to get out of here fast."

John had left the engine running, and they both jumped into the small craft. Dakota must have informed him that they needed to make a quick getaway. The boat seated four people and was open.

"Where to?" asked John.

Dakota looked over his shoulder. "Just get us out of here. Dock at the first safe place."

Grace glanced up the shore as well. Blondie and Randy were surveying the boats in the harbor. They were probably going to take an empty boat or acquire one at gunpoint.

John backed out of the dock and headed toward open water. They had to pass through a narrow inlet where tree-lined shores jutted out from the land. The Seattle skyline was in the distance.

"Where to now?" said John.

Dakota pressed close to Grace to be heard above the clang of the motor. "Do you think if we talked to Henry in person, he would believe us?"

"I don't know," said Grace. "I didn't get a picture of Elise with Justin Wilson. We don't have any evidence."

"And my guess is that Elise will put all her energy into getting rid of us first. It might be that after we're gone, Henry will look into things."

"I don't want to have to die for this case to be resolved." She peered over her shoulder. Another boat had pulled out of the dock and was heading in their direction. The boat was gaining on them and coming directly toward them.

"Sorry this thing can't go any faster," said John.

The boat Blondie and Randy had stolen or hijacked was larger and faster, with an enclosed area for the driver.

The boat narrowed the distance between them, drawing within thirty feet. She could see Randy manning the boat and Blondie had come out on the bow. Though he had not drawn his gun yet, she suspected he was waiting to get close enough to line up a shot.

"John, you better get low," said Dakota.

"Not to worry," said John. "I have an idea. This boat is slow, but it's more agile than that behemoth that is after us."

John turned sharply in the water and headed toward a cluster of sailboats. He wove in and out of them. The thugs' boat drew close but was only able to circle around the others. John headed toward a distant harbor The other boat came toward them but was unable to close the distance between them before they got to the dock. Dakota jumped out and tied off the boat, Grace was right behind him.

"Thanks for the ride," said Dakota.

John glanced out toward the water as the boat that held Randy and Blondie approached the dock. "Do you need my help with anything else? This looks kind of serious."

Dakota stepped toward his friend and patted his shoulder. "You've done enough. I don't want to put you in harm's way."

John reached out his hand to grip Dakota's and pat his shoulder. "Stay safe, brother."

"I'll be back at work before you know it," said Dakota.

Grace hoped that was true.

They were halfway up the shore when the other boat came in to dock. Blondie and Randy would be able to see where they had gone and follow them. The crowds of people provided a degree of protection.

"Can you call Henry and see if he'll meet with us? You said you trusted Henry. We have to convince him to at least bring Elise in for questioning if she hasn't already escaped."

Grace nodded. Dakota was trying to come up with a plan. Her mind had been spinning as well ever since she'd seen Justin and Elise together. "What if Elise has Henry's phone bugged? She might find a way to stop us before we can see him face-to-face."

They moved toward the street where there were shops and outdoor cafés and more people milling around than there had been at the other side of the harbor. This area of the shore connected with greater Seattle and was much more populated. In one direction she could see Gas Works Park and in the other was the city high-rises.

Grace peered over her shoulder and looked down the shore. Randy and Blondie were headed toward them.

"Do you think Elise and Justin will try to leave the country?" she asked.

"They might, but I think their first option would be to try to take us out since we're the only ones who know what is really going on."

"I'd like to live to see justice served," she said. She noticed several police officers at the end of the block. A thought occurred to her. Blondie and Randy were just hired muscle. They had mentioned not getting paid until she and Dakota were dead. As long as they were being hounded by those two, it would be impossible to figure out how to clear their names and see that Elise and Justin were brought to justice. "Come on, I have an idea." She walked a little faster.

Sure enough, Randy and Blondie split up but continued to follow them.

Dakota was right behind her as she approached the police officers. "Excuse me, sir. Those two men." She pointed first to Randy and then to Blondie. "They threatened my husband and I with guns."

Randy took a step back, shrinking into the crowd when one of the police officers looked in his direction.

Dakota addressed the second officer. "They both have guns, and they threatened us with them."

"We'll check it out," said the first officer as he stepped away from them and strode toward Blondie.

Blondie turned and took off running, as did Randy when the second officer headed toward him.

The third police officer addressed Grace and Dakota. "I'm going to need your names and phone numbers just in case we have any questions."

While Dakota spoke to the officer, Grace watched as one of the officers caught up with Randy. The other chased Blondie around a corner. Hopefully, he would be caught. In any case, he would be on the run and not able to follow Grace and Dakota. The men could be held for twenty-four hours without being charged with anything. Hopefully, they would be charged with at least brandishing a firearm.

Once the third officer walked away, Grace tugged on Dakota's sleeve. "We have to try to find Henry. It's Friday, and I know he goes to his houseboat a lot for a long weekend."

Dakota nodded. "We don't have much time. Once those thugs are taken into custody, I'm sure their first phone call will be to Elise or Justin."

They flagged down a taxi and sped toward where Henry kept his houseboat. Hopefully, he was still in the harbor. Otherwise, they were out of options. They might be forced to go into hiding until they came up with a way to clear their names and prove to DEA that they were not the guilty party and there was no longer a target on their backs.

From the back seat of the taxi where he sat with Grace, Dakota grew more tense as traffic on the expressway slowed to a crawl.

"Must be an accident," said the taxi driver.

Dakota lifted his head to see above the seat. Up ahead, he saw the flashing lights of an ambulance and other first responders.

Every minute counted. Grace was right about the two
men probably alerting Elise or Justin once they were in
custody and could make their phone call. Trying to find
Henry was the obvious move. What if he wasn't even
on the houseboat? They'd be left to play hide-and-seek
through the city until they could convince someone in
authority that it was not them who were involved in
the drug trade.

Traffic came to a complete standstill.

Seeing the look of fear that came over Grace, Dakota reached over and grabbed her hand. They were in
this together.

"There is no way around this?"

"Not at this point," said the taxi driver. "If we could
move just a little more, I'd be able to get off on that exit
and drive through the city."

Dakota closed his eyes and prayed. When he opened
them, he saw that Grace was doing the same thing, eyes
closed, lips moving.

They waited another five minutes before traffic
started moving again. A lot of blinkers were on, indicating that many people had the same idea of taking the exit. The taxi driver slipped over two lanes and
signaled. Once they were on the exit, traffic was still
moving slowly because of the amount of people who
had taken the exit.

"We are five minutes away from the harbor, but it
might take us fifteen to get there," said Grace, tension
threading through her words.

When he got a chance, the taxi driver sped up and
soon arrived at the harbor. The accident had caused at
least a twenty-minute delay. Dakota paid him and they
got out of the cab. The harbor where Henry kept his

houseboat was a small private one, surrounded by trees that blocked the view of the city, though they could still hear the sound of traffic and see the taller buildings above the tree line.

There were four other boats in the dock, but no sign of any other people.

Henry was not visible on the deck of his houseboat. Dakota feared that the delay in getting over to the harbor would have given Elise a chance to send someone to take them out.

Grace grabbed Dakota's arm. "What if he's not here?"

"Only one way to find out," said Dakota. They stalked toward the houseboat. Through the windows, he couldn't see any movement.

Grace hung back on the shore while Dakota stepped onto the deck of the boat. "Henry?" He peered into the first window, which provided a view of the kitchen. No one was there. He walked around to the side of the houseboat and peered through the window that had a view of the sleeping quarters. Henry lay on the bed on his side, motionless. Dakota's throat squeezed tight. Was he sleeping, dead or drugged?

Grace stepped toward him. "What is it?"

A noise off to the side drew Dakota's attention. The cover of the boat next to the houseboat was thrown off. Justin stood up and aimed a gun at Dakota. The red dot of the laser gun sight landed on his chest.

TWENTY

Grace watched in horror as Justin took aim at Dakota, the man she still loved. Dakota dove to the deck of the houseboat and crawled on all fours to get to the other side. The side that faced the shore where she was. The first shot shattered the window.

Grace sought cover, racing toward the trees. Elise popped up from inside the boat on the opposite side from where Justin was. She aimed her gun at Grace just as she slipped behind a tree.

Grace had just hidden in the trees when Elise climbed out of the boat and headed toward her.

Her heart raced as she heard footsteps behind her. She wove through the thick of forest in an erratic pattern until she stepped out onto a country road. Behind her, she heard two shots but the sounds were farther away—not from Elise's gun. Her heart squeezed tight. Had Justin shot Dakota?

Her breathing became even more shallow as she pushed aside the images of Dakota dying. She ran along the road and then back into the trees until she could hear the sound of water breaking on the shore.

She could also hear Elise running through the trees

behind her. Grace sprinted a short distance up the shore and then back through the forest that led to the road. She suspected she was in better shape than Elise. If she turned the pursuit into an endurance race, she might have a fighting chance.

Once she was on the gravel road, she ran. She could hear the sounds of traffic above her on the highway that had brought them to the secluded harbor. She sprinted along the shoulder of the road. She peered over her shoulder. No sign of Elise. If she had a moment, she would at least be able to call the police and tell them there had been a shooting incident. How long would it take for them to arrive? Twenty minutes. Her hand brushed over the phone she had in her jacket pocket. When she looked behind her, Elise had just come up on the road. No time to call the police.

All Grace had to do was keep the distance between them to make sure Elise couldn't fire off an accurate shot.

Grace slipped back into the brush that led downhill. She ran back into the trees. She could not see or hear the sounds of the harbor. It was hard to judge how far away she was.

Again, she thought of Dakota. What had those shots been about? Was he lying in a pool of his own blood? If that was the case, then Justin would be looking for her too. The smart thing to do would be to keep working her way away from the harbor until she could call for help and wait, but she could not let go of the idea that she needed to get to Dakota. What if he needed her help?

She was torn. Dakota had known the risk when he'd taken the assignment. The agent part of her knew that the best strategy was to put distance between herself and her pursuer and call the police. But the part of her that realized she still loved Dakota knew she wanted to be with him and said she needed to go to him regardless, even if it meant she'd be caught and killed.

She worked her way in the general direction that she thought the harbor was. Human noises behind her caused her to seek cover behind a tree. She pressed her back against the bark. Her heartbeat drummed in her ears. She heard more sounds. Someone walking through the forest. She leaned out to peer around the tree. Some distance away, she caught a glimpse of color. Elise stalking through the forest, searching and moving away from where Grace was hiding.

Grace waited, feeling the roughness of the tree bark where her palm pressed against it. Elise's back was to her. She might be able to jump the other woman. Crouching, she moved forward, hiding behind another tree and moving toward the other woman.

She glanced side to side, aware that Justin might be searching for her as well. Her eyes scanned the trees and brush. Seeing nothing out of place, she strode forward, treading lightly and watching for branches on the ground or anything that would make noise.

The lush green forest provided ample cover for her and she surged forward, closing the distance between herself and Elise. Elise still held her gun up, ready to shoot, then stopped for a moment.

Grace crouched down, peering through the green of the bush she hid behind. Elise turned one way and then the other. She must have sensed that she was being followed.

Grace's heart pounded as sweat formed on her forehead. She waited for the moment when Elise's back was fully toward her before she jumped up from her hiding place. It took three large strides to sprint to where Elise was. Elise turned halfway. Her mouth gaped when she saw Grace coming toward her. She raised the gun just as Grace tackled her. The shot went off to the side, but Elise held on to the gun.

Grace dove for the gun, hoping to restrain her before she could shoot again. Elise bared her teeth at Grace as she lifted her gun. "You should have been dead by now."

"I don't think so, Elise." A voice came at her from the side. Dakota held a gun at Elise. "Drop the gun right now."

Elise's glance moved from Grace to Dakota as her face grew red with rage. She must be weighing her options. "I could just shoot her, you know." She addressed her remark to Dakota but was still looking at Grace.

"You could," said Dakota. "But then I could shoot you. Drop the gun, Elise."

Elise complied.

"Get the gun, Grace." Grace lifted her knees, which had been resting on Elise's stomach to subdue her. She grabbed the gun and got to her feet, aiming the gun at Elise.

Relief and love flooded through Grace in equal measure. "When I heard those shots, I thought for sure I'd lost you."

"No, Grace. I'm not going anywhere." Dakota shook his head. "I remembered that Henry always kept a gun on his houseboat. I was able to get to it before Justin got inside."

"Justin?" Elise cried out.

"He's alive and tied up. The shot I fired nicked his

leg. An ambulance is on its way." Dakota gestured for Elise to stand up.

"What about Henry?"

"He's breathing but unresponsive. I think he was drugged so a trap could be set for us."

Elise stumbled to her feet.

"Keep your hands in the air and walk back to the boat," said Dakota. Grace and Dakota walked side by side, both keeping their guns and eyes on Elise.

In the distance, she heard the shrill cry of sirens. The ambulance and other first responders were on the way.

They marched Elise back to the boat and tied her up as well while they waited for the ambulance and local police. Justin sat on the floor of the houseboat. His pant leg was bloody where Dakota must have nicked him. Henry was just coming to when the EMTs showed up to check on him.

The EMTs dealt with Justin's wound as well.

Grace approached the local police, explaining that Elise and Justin had tried to kill them. "This is all connected to a DEA investigation that I think will be wrapped up soon." Grace pointed toward the ambulance where Henry was being treated. "That older man, Agent Henry Ward, will be able to fill you in on the details."

The police officer went over to question Henry.

Henry and Justin were transported in separate ambulances.

Dakota stood beside Grace.

"I was worried about you," said Dakota. "Don't know what I would do if you weren't in my life."

Responding to the intensity of his words, she glanced at him. Her heart beat a little faster. "What are you saying?"

"I'm just saying, I want you in my life." He locked his gaze on her "You decide what that looks like."

Grace's mouth fell open. She wasn't sure what to say.

There had been two police cars. The first one had hauled Elise away. The remaining officer walked over to them. "I can give you two a ride."

Dakota gave the location of the parking garage where they had left Wilson's rental car. As they drove through the city, Dakota's words echoed through her head. She did love him. He was not the man who had hurt her so deeply three years ago. But what did that mean for the two of them? There was still so much pain to work through. "I think we should be the ones to let Mr. Wilson know what his son was involved in."

"We would have to clear that with Henry first."

"Of course. Why don't we leave the rental at the hotel with a message that we can't continue in his employment right now," she said. "If Henry gives the okay, we'll get in touch with Mr. Wilson."

The police officer dropped them off at the parking garage. They sat silently in the car while Dakota drove back to the hotel. They left the car with the message for Mitchell Wilson. Dakota was able to make some calls to associates in the police department. Randy and Blondie were both in custody pending further charges.

They walked along a path beside a park in the waning light of early evening. Her hand slipped into his. "I've been thinking that maybe it's time for a change."

He stopped and faced her. "What are you saying?"

"For one thing, I don't want to do undercover work anymore. I'm thinking maybe it would be more life-giving to be a chef."

"I like that idea, Gracie." He leaned a little closer to her. "What about us?"

"Dakota, I love you. You are different. God has changed you, but I'm afraid we have all this bad history."

"I'm afraid too." He placed his hand on her cheek. "Let's be afraid together and just take it real slow."

"That is the optimal word, isn't it? *Together*. Whatever the future holds for us, good or bad, we need to face it together."

"Yes, together...no matter what. I love you too, Grace." He leaned in and kissed her.

His arms wrapped around her and he drew her close. Relishing the comfort and safety of the arms of the man she loved, Grace tilted her head to look into his eyes. He kissed her again. And she knew in her heart that this time with God's help they could rebuild their lives...together.

* * * * *

If you enjoyed this story,
look for these other books by Sharon Dunn:

Mountain Captive
Wilderness Secrets
In Too Deep

Dear Reader,

I hope you enjoyed reading about Dakota and Grace and how they faced danger together and found a renewed love for each other. As with all my books, I have favorite scenes. I think the scene early in the book where Grace nearly drowns and cries out to a God she has never spoken to before is one I really like. Though she is in physical danger, the scene in a way represents where we have all been at one time or another in a symbolic way. We have all felt overwhelmed and like we might drown emotionally, either because of finances or health or family problems or just a to-do list that never gets shorter. At the beginning of this book, I included the verse from Jonah because it was such a perfect picture of how God hears us when we're drowning, and we cry out to Him. Feeling overwhelmed today? Cry out to God; He will answer.

Thanks,
Sharon Dunn

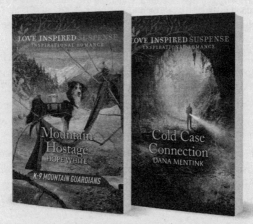

COMING NEXT MONTH FROM
Love Inspired Suspense

Available June 2, 2020

DEADLY CONNECTION
True Blue K-9 Unit: Brooklyn • by Lenora Worth
On her way to question US Marshal Emmett Gage about a DNA match that implicates someone in his family in a cold case tied to a recent murder, Brooklyn K-9 officer Belle Montera is attacked. Now she must team up with Emmett to find the killer...before she becomes the next victim.

PLAIN REFUGE
Amish Country Justice • by Dana R. Lynn
After overhearing an illegal gun deal, Sophie Larson's sure of two things: her uncle's a dangerous crime boss...and he wants her dead. With a mole in the police force and Sophie in danger, undercover cop Aiden Forster has no choice but to blow his cover and hide her deep in Amish country.

SECRETS RESURFACED
Roughwater Ranch Cowboys • by Dana Mentink
When new evidence surfaces that the man her ex-boyfriend's father was accused of drowning is still alive, private investigator Dory Winslow's determined to find him. But working with Chad Jaggert—the father of her secret daughter—wasn't part of her plan. Can they survive the treacherous truth about the past?

TEXAS TWIN ABDUCTION
Cowboy Lawmen • by Virginia Vaughan
Waking up in a bullet-ridden car with a bag of cash and a deputy insisting she's his ex, Ashlee Taylor has no memory of what happened—or of Lawson Avery. But he's the only one she trusts as they try to restore her memory...and find her missing twin.

STOLEN CHILD
by Jane M. Choate
On leave from his deployment, army ranger Grey Nighthorse must track down his kidnapped daughter. But when he's shot at as soon as his investigation begins, he needs backup. And hiring former FBI agent Rachel Martin is his best chance at staying alive long enough to recover his little girl.

JUSTICE UNDERCOVER
by Connie Queen
Presumed-dead ex-US Marshal Kylie Stone goes undercover as a nanny for Texas Ranger Luke Dryden to find out who killed his sister—and the witness who'd been under Kylie's protection. But when someone tries to kidnap the twins in her care, she has to tell Luke the truth...and convince him to help her.

_____

LOOK FOR THESE AND OTHER LOVE INSPIRED BOOKS WHEREVER BOOKS ARE SOLD, INCLUDING MOST BOOKSTORES, SUPERMARKETS, DISCOUNT STORES AND DRUGSTORES.

LISCNM0520

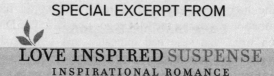
Brooklyn K-9 Unit officer Belle Montera glanced back on the shortcut through Cadman Plaza Park, her K-9 partner, Justice, a sleek German shepherd, moving ahead of her as she held tightly to his leash. She had a weird sense she was being followed, but it had to be nothing.

Justice lifted his black nose and sniffed the humid air, then gave a soft woof. He might have seen a squirrel frolicking in the tall oaks, or he could have sensed Belle's agitation. Still on duty, she kept a keen eye on her surroundings.

"No time to go after innocent squirrels," she told Justice. "We're working, remember?"

Her faithful companion gave her a dark-eyed stare, his black K-9 unit protective vest cinched around his firm belly.

They were both on high alert.

"It's okay, boy," she said, giving Justice's shiny black-and-tan coat a soft rub. "Just my overactive imagination getting the best of me."

She had a meeting with a man who could have information regarding the McGregor murders. The DNA match from that case had indicated that US marshal Emmett Gage could be related to the killer.

The team had done a thorough background check on the marshal to eliminate him as a suspect, then Belle had been assigned to meet with him.

Justice lifted his head and sniffed again, his nose in the air. The big dog glanced back. Belle checked over her shoulder.

No one there.

She slowed and listened to hear if any footsteps hit the strip of pavement curving through the path toward the federal courthouse near the park.

Belle heard through the trees what sounded like a motorcycle revving, then nothing but the birds chirping. Minutes passed and then she heard a noise on the path, the crackle of a twig breaking, the slight shift of shoes hitting asphalt, a whiff of stale body odor wafting through the air. The hair on the back of her neck stood up and Belle knew then.

Someone is following me.

Don't miss
Deadly Connection *by Lenora Worth,*
available June 2020 wherever
Love Inspired Suspense books and ebooks are sold.

LoveInspired.com

USA TODAY bestselling author

SHEILA ROBERTS

returns with the next book in her irresistible Moonlight Harbor series, set on the charming Washington coast.

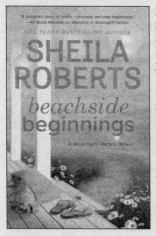

Moira Wellman has always loved makeovers—helping women find their most beautiful selves. Funny how it's taken her five years with her abusive boyfriend, Lang, to realize she needs a life makeover. When Moira finally gets the courage to leave Lang, the beachside town of Moonlight Harbor is the perfect place to start her new life.

Soon Moira is right at home, working as a stylist at Waves Salon, making new friends, saving her clients from beauty blunders and helping the women of Moonlight Harbor find the confidence to take back their lives. When she meets a handsome police officer, she's more than willing to give him a free haircut. Maybe even her heart. But is she really ready for romance after Lang? And what if her new friend is in hot pursuit of that same cop? This is worse than a bad perm. Life surely can't get any more difficult. Or can it?

With all the heart and humor readers have come to expect from a Sheila Roberts novel, *Beachside Beginnings* is the story of one woman finding the courage to live her best life. And where better to live it than at the beach?

Coming soon from MIRA books.

Be sure to connect with us at:
Harlequin.com/Newsletters
Facebook.com/HarlequinBooks
Twitter.com/HarlequinBooks

mira

Harlequin.com

MSR089

SPECIAL EXCERPT FROM

Arlene had left and Pearl had just finished trimming Jo's hair when the bell over the door of Waves Salon jingled and in walked Edie Patterson followed by a woman, who was the image of young and hip, holding a cat carrier.

"Whoa," said Jo, looking at her.

Whoa was right. The girl wore the latest style in jeans. Her jacket and gray sweater, while not high-end quality, were equally stylish. She had a tiny gold hoop threaded through one nostril, and when she flipped her hair aside part of a butterfly tattoo showed on her neck. Her features were pretty and her makeup beautifully done. And that hair. She had glorious hair—long, shimmery and luminescent like a pearl or the inside of an oyster shell. The colors were magical.

This had to be the woman Michael had sent down. Either that or she was a gift from the hair gods. She looked around the salon, taking it all in.

Pearl saw the flash of disappointment in her eyes and suddenly knew how exposed Adam and Eve must have felt after they ate that forbidden fruit. *Adam, we're naked!* Looking at her little salon through the newcomer's eyes, she saw all the things that had become invisible to her over the years: the pink shampoo bowls, old Formica styling stations, posters on the walls showing dated hairstyles like mullets and feathered bangs. The walls were the same dull cream color they'd been when Pearl had first bought the place. And the ancient linoleum floor…ugh. The place looked tired and old. With the exception of Chastity and Tyrella Lamb, who was getting her nails done, so did the women in it.

MEXPSR089

The newcomer quickly covered her disappointment with an uncertain smile.

"Hello, Pearl," said Edie. "I met this nice young lady at Nora's. She's come here looking for a job."

The woman barely waited for Edie to finish before walking up to Pearl and holding out her hand. "Hi. I'm Moira Wellman."

Determined and polite. It made a good first impression. "I'm Pearl Edwards. Michael told me you were coming."

Insecurity surfaced. The girl caught her lower lip between her teeth. "Do you have an opening? I'm good with hair," she added.

"I'm sure you are or Michael wouldn't have sent you," Pearl said. She was aware of Jo seated in her chair, taking in every word. "I tell you what. I've got a Keurig in the back room. Help yourself to some coffee and I'll be with you in just a few minutes. Okay?"

Moira nodded, picked up the cat carrier and slipped through the curtain that separated the salon from the back, where Pearl kept her supplies and washer and dryer and a small break area.

"I didn't know you were hiring someone," Jo said as Pearl returned to finish with her hair.

Pearl hadn't known she was hiring anyone, either.

Before she could speak, Chastity said, "I love her hair. I wonder if she could do that to mine."

That decided it. "I think it's time I did some updating," Pearl said.

Find out what happens next in
Beachside Beginnings
*by Sheila Roberts, available April 2020 wherever
MIRA books and ebooks are sold.*

MIRABooks.com